Cherish the Day

When Love Somehow Finds Its Way

Olivia Almagro

K.A.M'S PUBLISHING COMPANY LLC

ISBN: 978-1-7373337-6-0

K.A.M.'s Publishing

Los Angeles, CA 90008

www.kimamorrow.com

I dedicate this book to my dear friends the

late Erica Tinker and Joy Rambert.

Proverbs 3:15 She is more precious than rubies;

nothing you desire can compare with her.

Table of Contents

Acknowledgements: i

Chapter 1: Crooklyn 3

Chapter 2: Waiting to Exhale 12

Chapter 3: Why Do Fools Fall in Love 22

Chapter 4: Love Jones 31

Chapter 5: Lady Sings the Blues 38

Chapter 6: A Thin Line Between Love and Hate.......46

Chapter 7: Eve's Bayou...52

Chapter 8: Above the Rim.......................................65

Chapter 9: Which Way is Up 73

Chapter 10: Uptown Saturday Night 80

Chapter 11: She's Gotta Have It 91

Chapter 12: Jason's Lyric 97

Chapter 13: Antoine Fisher 104

Chapter 14: Mahogany 111

Chapter 15: Claudine...118

Chapter 16: Jason's Lyric 126

Chapter 17: The Best Man 135

Chapter 18: Trading Places 144

Chapter 19: Dream Girls 153

Chapter 20: Red Tails 160

Chapter 21: Krush Groove 170

Chapter 22: Hurricane 179

Chapter 23: The Pursuit of Happiness 186

Acknowledgements:

Father God – I thank You for all that You do. I wouldn't be half the woman I am today without Your presence in my life. I praise You, in Jesus' name. Amen.

To my parents, Charles A. Brown and Alicia Almagro – I miss you so much. There is not a day that goes by that I am not thinking of you with a huge smile on my face. I am so blessed to have had you in my life. I love you. Until we meet again.

My oldest sister Alicia Zayas, the matriarch of the family – I love you dearly. Thank you for being my protector.

John Almagro – Thank you, my older brother, for always being there for me and believing in me. I don't know what I would do without you. Love, Your Little Sister.

To my brother Robert Almagro Sr., my sports and political sparring match – I love you dearly!

To my besties, Kimberly A. Morrow and Dr. Stacie A. Morris – Thank you for being the inspiration to my characters in Cherish The Day. Your friendship means the world to me and I am so blessed to be on this journey called life with you. Love you always.

Ms. Tinker – I appreciate you and thank you for giving us our sister and friend Erica.

Chanel Taylor – To my sister from another mother. Thank you for putting up with me. You're my second brain and my mathematician. Thank you for always being by my side and telling me when I am wrong.

Eva Jane Bunkley – My sister-friend. I am so proud of you. I think you know that already. Thank you for supporting me all these years. I love you!

Anna Mariotti – Thank you for being my friend. I think back on all the fun times we had working together in Hartford. We laughed so much. We are like kindred spirits. I don't tell you often, but I appreciate our friendship. Love you!

My cousin Caroline Brown from the UK – My cousin who I adore and love. I am truly enjoying this ride called life with you. Love you!

Karen McLean – Thank you for always being there for me. I got your back.

My childhood friend Tiffany whom I named my character after – I love you, and thank you for being constant in my life.

To my childhood friend and sister Verlecuia "Lisa" Mitchell – Partly the reason I was born. Inside joke. Thank you for your support. Love you dearly!

Larry McColley, my fellow Brownite and brother, whose good looks and charm inspired my character – I truly appreciate you and value our friendship.

Jeffrey Miller – Thank you for being a trusted friend.

Sheila – You do amazing graphic design! I appreciate you. All Hail to the Queen.

My editor, Gina Casto – Thank you so much for your invaluable support. I truly appreciate you and all that you do.

Upper Albany Neighborhood Collaborative Family – Thank you for your support!

My Morris Brown College Family and The Atlanta University Center – Thank you for an incredible journey during undergrad and for being the backdrop of my story.

Chapter 1

Crooklyn

Leaving Brooklyn felt surreal, like waking up from a long dream. The noise, the grit, the relentless hustle wore me down mentally. I wasn't chasing the American dream anymore—I was running from it.

Brooklyn is a far cry from what it once was. The smell of jerk from Caribbean takeout and roti restaurants used to fill every corner in Flatbush, and dancehall music blared from huge speakers planted outside clothing and check-cashing stores. Even the storefront churches reverberating to the sounds of calypso-inspired gospel music made this community one of a kind.

Norstrand and Fulton Avenues still held on strong while hopes remained high that these streets would remain true to their cultural identities and not be influenced by gentrification. Though I was surely going to miss it, this country gal from Snowville, North Carolina, decided it was time to say goodbye to New York City. The mid-sized tech company I had been working for as a software engineer for five years was bought out by a competitor, so I happily accepted my severance package, and they offered a one-year contract to work remotely with the transition team.

Everything was going according to my plan to set off on an adventure of self-discovery, experiencing a new culture, possibly love, and a new way of living in Costa Rica.

I ended the evening at a cozy pub, tearfully saying goodbye to a circle of friends in Brooklyn. We spent an evening filled with moments of laughter, joy, and sadness while the conversations kept coming around to the one topic: I tried hard to avoid my love life.

The elephant in the room hovered over me, everyone wondering why I had not found that special someone yet. I didn't have an answer for them, and judging by their reactions, I got the impression that they somehow believed I was at fault for being single. Why else would I still be alone?

I took pride in the fact that I had dated a decent number of men in the past while most of my friends in Brooklyn were either married or in committed relationships. I held onto the belief that when the time was right, the right person would come along. I had to trust in the timing of God and have faith that my future love was out there, even if we hadn't crossed paths yet.

While I guarded those words closely, our conversations lingered in my mind like a lonely shadow, slowly chipping away at my confidence as I rode the subway home, lost in my thoughts.

Over the past twelve months, the extent of my romantic life involved a few possible suitors: a lawyer, an Amazon delivery driver and several years before that, I had a brief fling with a coworker originally from DR, aka my Latin lover. We were still friendly and occasionally kept in touch through texts.

I could not forget a current interest, Tyrone from the Boogie Down Bronx—yes, you read it correctly—whom I met through a mutual friend. We'd gone on a few dates but were taking it slow, and I was also sort of dating a few others online, just to keep my options open.

Though I didn't take those relationships too seriously, it was nice to connect with someone from time to time. Besides, I craved companionship. Some of the men stood taller than six feet, others just shy of it, a requirement I stood by with bodies ranging from chiseled frames to potbellies. They came from everywhere: the Caribbean, the Middle East, South Sudan, Eastern Europe, New Jersey, and from the deep South to the heartland—all finding their way to my hemisphere.

They were corporate slayers, techies on the brink of disruptive change, hardworking wage-earners putting in their hours, and, of course, I'd be remiss not to mention a few deadbeats in the mix. Some were bold, others more subtle. A few entered my life like a whirlwind, sweeping me off my feet, while others lingered quietly, like a slow-burning fire on the verge of erupting. With every encounter, my life twisted and turned in ways I couldn't have imagined. Yet, each one brought their own unique style to the art of dating, keeping my life anything but predictable.

I checked my messages and saw that James, the Amazon delivery guy, wanted to meet up for drinks in Soho. The attorney, Carl, had checked in by text. He was preparing for trial and wanted to meet up for a quick bite to eat. With the movers arriving first thing in the morning, my focus was on finishing my last-minute packing and getting the hell out of Dodge.

I did not expect to feel sad about not seeing them anymore once I moved away. After all, I had no strong connection with any of those men, and I did not feel the slightest bit of regret for not saying goodbye in person. Besides, I wanted a man who would make me feel safe and secure to the point where I could close my eyes and confidently trust him to be there to catch me when I fell. Someone who would worship the ground I walked on while understanding that I'm not perfect, but I am more than enough for him.

The next morning, I walked through my tiny one-bedroom walkup apartment, checking drawers and closets for anything overlooked by either me or the movers, but nothing remained, and the empty space echoed this truth.

Releasing a deep sigh, I juggled all four suitcases to the street and then loaded them into my BMW. There was something oddly satisfying about the sound of them clacking and bumping against each other. It was music to my ears. One final look in my rearview mirror confirmed that it was time to embark on that new adventure.

***

For once, I didn't wake up to honking car horns, sirens, noisy trains traveling through a busy subway tunnel and people bustling about. I woke up to paradise, where the sun's rays shone down on my cocoa brown skin, instantly dragging me from my sleep.

I realized I wasn't dreaming when I heard exotic birds chirping and breathed in the salty smell of the ocean in the air just outside my bedroom window. The fresh scent of lavender from the supplies used to clean the villa was an added touch that stirred all my senses.

With all my belongings neatly stowed away, it already felt like home. I even managed to scatter the few photos of my friends and family I'd brought along around the villa, making it cozier.

My excitement reached its peak when I received a message from the concierge that Maverick, my eight-month-old Rottweiler, was about to arrive. All my thoughts drifted to the cozy afternoons we spent in Brooklyn, cuddled on the couch, munching on trail mix while watching reruns of *A Different World*.

My heart raced, and joy overwhelmed me as I opened the door and Maverick came running toward me at full speed with his leash trailing behind him and dragging on to the floor.

"Tiffany Myers?" asked the male attendant, who stood awkwardly at the top of the steps. I tumbled onto the tile floor from Maverick's sheer force, and he proceeded to lick my face over and over again.

After regaining composure, I replied, "Yes, that's me." I quickly scribbled my signature on the receipt and handed it to the attendant, along with a twenty-dollar tip, before taking a moment with Maverick.

As I watched Maverick run around and explore our new home, I was overcome with a deep sense of happiness. This was exactly what I had been waiting for.

The day was still young as I stepped out wearing a mandarin yellow sleeveless cotton dress that tugged on my hips and butt. It fell slightly above my ankles, only exposing my well-manicured toes in my tortoiseshell leather sandals. I was looking good if I did have to say so myself, and even the Yoruba Goddess Oshun would agree.

The glaring sun pierced right through my dress and exposed my nipples and a silhouette of my body. My tightly coiled 4C hair that rested past my shoulders and toward the middle of my back was tucked away in a head wrap, a few of my baby hairs peeking out, with the help of some great edge control I bought from the Duane Reade drugstore, framing my face. My gold hoops that bore my name in the center completed the look.

As I walked along the road heading to the market, I felt a sense of emotional freedom like never before. The warm breeze caressed my body as I swung my arm around and swayed my hips with the rhythm of the summer breeze, feeling truly alive and at peace now. The stares from the locals served as a reminder that they, too, were witnessing happiness at its peak and my dramatic transformation before them.

The scene at the market was alive with vibrant colors and strong smells, like the sharp tang of ginger and garlic. The romantic sound of Bachata music added to the robust energy of the market, and the sweet smell of papaya brought me closer to the produce section, the shiny, crimson-colored tomatoes catching my attention.

Everywhere I looked, there were stacks of fruits and vegetables on tables and people haggling over prices. I took my time walking past each vendor, amazed at the different varieties of fish and seafood on display.

It wasn't until I reached the end of the market that I realized just how many culinary treasures I had seen in such a short span of time. I even discovered herbs I had never heard of before and tasted things I never knew existed.

I left with bags filled with all the necessary ingredients, my mind full of ideas for exotic dishes I could create. As I walked toward home, my attention was drawn to a beautiful couple, their hands intertwined as they jointly held a single basket. The man had salt-and-pepper mangled locks that reached below his waist, and he wore a white linen shirt and slacks to complement the look. The woman had huge coils that sprang out from everywhere on her head and wore a white fitted off-the-shoulder sundress, the print adorned with huge, colorful flowers. Their Hershey-colored hues were so beautiful that it took my breath away, the two of them looking as if they had been plucked from Paris Fashion Week. Without hesitation, I quickly pulled out my camera and began to capture the moment.

From a distance, their round lips seemed to move in sync and in slow motion, clinging to each other's every word. My gaze couldn't help but be drawn to these two as they leisurely strolled along the embankment, and the sight became etched into my mind. A part of me yearned for that type of attention from a man. I nurtured a dream that, eventually, I would come across someone who would cherish me in that same way. But I was doubtful at times that it would ever happen.

***

I set up a makeshift darkroom inside my second bathroom, closest to the backdoor leading out to the patio. I lifted the prints to a crimson light, revealing beautiful images of the couple I had seen earlier. As I stared intently at the photos, I sensed the love shared between the two. The way they looked at each other and the way they held hands was a testament to their deep connection. A bit of envy came over me as I yearned to have someone to share that kind of love with, but I quickly shook off the feeling and focused on the task at hand. The prints were perfect, and I couldn't wait to add them to my collection of photos.

Emotionally drained, I lounged on my bed. My mind kept racing back to the couple. I craved intimacy, and I wanted so badly at that moment to be held by a man. However, not just any man. A special someone whom I could share my innermost secrets with, laugh with, and trust completely.

My mind filled with a yearning for Mr. Feel Good, my battery-powered pink contraption that promised a satisfaction guarantee. I began caressing my rounded breasts and chocolate-coated nipples that emerged from the stroke of my hand. I became instantly wet, my inner walls swelling with desire. The buzzing and movement of Mr. Feel Good inside me sent orgasmic shockwaves throughout my entire body and, hell, even my toes.

Afterward, I lay still with my eyes closed for long minutes. The sound of the wind outside rustling the banana trees was strangely calming. Every muscle in my body loosened, and I allowed myself to experience the moment. A sense of peace filled me, and my earlier thoughts slowly began to fade as I drifted off.

Maverick's loud chewing and consistent panting disturbed my sleep. After hours of his incessant noise, I dragged myself out of bed, determined to find out what had caught Maverick's attention. To my surprise, I found him seated in the doorway of my bedroom with Mr. Feel Good in his mouth. Around his prize, Maverick carried a cheerful, satisfied expression.

"No, Maverick," I shouted, but it was too late. Mr. Feel Good had been shredded to pieces. I peered into Maverick's throat to see if any more parts remained, and after removing a huge piece, Maverick whimpered. He seemed traumatized and bewildered by the excitement of my voice.

I had let both him and myself down. *Who would fill my emptiness now?* I considered getting a replacement, but I was too embarrassed to buy another one.

I snapped a few pictures of Mr. Feel Good in pieces and sent them to my best friends from college with the caption:

"Help! I'll clean for sex. LOL."

My phone immediately started buzzing, and before I knew it, I was on a video call with my college crew. We were all still in bed, wrapped in fluffy comforters, each of us sporting a colorful hair bonnet.

Roxanne was the first to ask, "What is that?"

"It's Mr. Feel Good," I replied.

"In pieces?" Hannah followed up, sounding shocked.

"Maverick got to it."

"That dog is something else." Roxanne laughed.

"Did you punish him?" Hannah asked.

"Yeah, but he's still a puppy."

"That's no excuse. He shouldn't be chewing your things," Elena added.

"So, what are you going to do now?" Roxanne asked.

"I'm too embarrassed to buy another one around here," I admitted.

"How do you say vibrator in Spanish?" Roxanne wondered.

We all burst out in laughter. "No idea," I said, still laughing.

"Well, take it as a sign that you need a man," Roxanne teased.

Hannah couldn't resist adding, "And nothing with batteries."

"You're on an island full of beautiful men. You should've ditched Mr. Feel Good in a Brooklyn dumpster," Roxanne joked.

"When we visit, you better be ready to hang out," Elena chimed in.

By the time we ended our call, I felt much better. My friends were right about one thing—it was a clear sign from the universe that it was time to make an effort to find someone new. Costa Rica wasn't just my new home—it was a clean slate. However, I did make a promise to myself that I wanted to be loved the right way and that there was no in-between or compromising anymore for the sake of having a man in my life.

If I couldn't have it the right way, I didn't want it at all.

Chapter 2

Waiting to Exhale

I sipped on my Moringa tea with honey and savored a bowl of açaí with papaya, granola and coconut blend as I virtually studied the tired faces and chapped lips of my colleagues. Dressed in sweaters up to their necks, they huddled around their laptops and updated their progress for the rest of the team.

For a while, my finger hovered over the "Leave Meeting" button as I thought of the refreshing yoga session I had planned at the beach. Seeing the look of exhaustion on my colleagues' faces brought back unwelcome memories of the same feelings I didn't miss.

"Can you provide us with an update, Joe," the lead team member asked. Covering at least half of his face with a mask, Joe was inadvertently cut off by the lead team member's erratic sneezing.

"Yes. I've emailed the work completed, and I estimate the backup system should be up and running by the end of the week."

"Great. Keep us posted," the lead said as he sneezed a dozen more times before ending the meeting.

***

I found it comforting to finally be outside, taking a few moments to soak in the sun and the ocean rolling against the sand. The tightness in my chest released as I slowly took deep breaths, matching the rhythm of the waves. I took a couple of sips of refreshing chilled cane juice I bought from a local street vendor and let my mind not think about work or deadlines.

I focused on bringing my attention back to the present moment. As I moved through the routine, I felt my worries slowly melt away. Melanie, the yoga instructor, stood in a circle around a patch of sand where her students had laid their mats with their arms outstretched.

Now exhale," she whispered, looking around at the assortment of ages of women gathered around her.

After yoga class, I felt more centered and at ease. I was grateful for the chance to relax and clear my mind before diving back into work mode.

I still had a few hours to spare, so I strolled through a strip of cafes and boutiques in the tourist part of town. Judging by the array of foreign languages I overheard, numerous nationalities were present.

I walked into a crowded gallery cafe and perused a catalog of contemporary and vintage artwork of prints and books. A rare print of Jean Michel Basquiat's self-portrait caught my attention.

As I looked up, I was surprised to see a good-looking man smiling at me from across the room. He approached, and my heart raced a mile a minute as I contemplated whether to make a run for the door or stay and hear him out.

"Hey, beautiful," he said, looking down into my eyes.

He reminded me of a younger version of NBA player Kyrie Irving, and his endearing, infectious smile could light up the entire Empire State Building in a single flash.

"Hello," I greeted the handsome man in front of me.

"I'm Malik Walker. And you are?"

My nerves were running high as his stunning presence had me temporarily forgetting my own name. After a moment, I managed to pull myself together enough to stammer out, "Tiffany Myers."

"Wait. You're not from here."

"No, I just moved here from New York City by way of North Carolina."

"Really? Wow. What a coincidence. I'm from Charlotte. I did my undergraduate at A&T."

With my nerves getting the best of me, I tucked a wisp of hair behind my ear. "I attended Morris Brown."

"Mo Brown, now that's what's up. Are you vacationing?"

"I actually live here."

"Nice."

We quickly found ourselves chatting like old friends. "How about you?" I asked.

"I'm contracted to be here for about a year. I'm an environmental scientist."

"What's that exactly?"

"My agency works with the local government to find ways to help prevent environmental damage. We collect data on issues like pollution and climate change."

He's smart! He has a doctorate in environmental science.

I couldn't help but also admire his attractiveness and impeccable physique. The fragrance of his cologne was a turn-on. *God, I'm not paying attention to anything he's telling me right now.* I stared back into his eyes and pretended to give him my full attention.

Then, I remembered I was on schedule. I looked down at my watch and realized I had just twenty minutes to hop on another work call. Panic began setting in, and judging by the concerned look in Malik's eyes, he noticed me worrying as well.

"Is everything alright?" he asked.

"I'm so sorry. It was nice to meet you," I replied before hastily darting for a cab.

After making it home, I learned the meeting had been canceled. I was disappointed when I realized Malik and I never exchanged numbers, and I might not see him again. I hated that I had to leave like a thief in the night.

I shrugged the thought away and decided to take advantage of my free afternoon. I turned on John Coltrane's "A Love Supreme" and soaked in a hot bath, cooked a delicious meal and poured myself a glass of Chardonnay. Then, I snuggled up with Maverick on the hammock, where we slept peacefully throughout the night.

I woke eager to get my day started, but not before heading off to the beach. Clinging to Maverick's worn leash, I pulled him clumsily down the sidewalk toward the ocean. As the sky lightened to a soft blue, we ran to the shore to witness the stunning beauty of the sunrise. I was captivated by the beautiful view.

"I'm in paradise," I `shouted to the world.

Maverick inched closer to the edge of the water as I watched the sun lift over the horizon and cast a yellow and orange glow across the sky. Moments later, small waves began to crash against the shore, and wildlife started to come alive as the new day broke.

Maverick was off his leash, and sensing freedom, he roamed aimlessly while I took in the sounds and smells of the beach. The peaceful roar of the waves, the salty air from the sea, and the faint scent of tropical flowers, including the national flower Guaria Morada from the new plants that lined the beach nearby.

I stopped here and there to find a few shells across the sand, feeling deeply connected to the ocean. It was as though Yemaya, an orisha and a powerful goddess of the sea, was drawing me in.

I was startled when I spotted a familiar face sprinting in my direction on the shore. As he came closer, Maverick started barking. It was Malik.

Won't he do it? I didn't know if I should break out in a holy dance, act a damn fool or remain cool, calm and collected.

"Hi!" Malik shouted and waved.

I quickly grabbed Maverick's collar and hurried over to him. When I finally reached him, the hug I gave Malik was one I didn't want to come undone.

He smiled at me and then looked down at Maverick by my side. Bending his tall frame, he asked curiously, "So, who is this big fella?" Maverick began sniffing and then started playing with him.

"This is Maverick," I said proudly. "What are you doing out here so early?"

"I'm out here most mornings taking a jog along the beach. You should join me sometime."

"Sure, but I'm not much of a jogger. I can speed walk, though."

"Then we'll speed walk."

I screamed out loud in my head.

Malik took hold of my hands, placed his fingers on mine and looked into my eyes. "Tiffany," do you believe in love at first sight?"

"No. I mean, I don't know." I chuckled as I shrugged.

"Would it be alright if I called you sometime? A dinner out together, perhaps? I know this may sound silly, but I haven't been able to stop thinking about you since I saw you at the cafe."

I wasn't sure if my mind was playing tricks on me, but regardless, I chose to take a chance. "I would love to."

"Cool. I need to head back and meet with my team in a short while."

We locked the other's number in our cell phones, then parted ways with a friendly goodbye, and he gave me a hug before continuing on his run. After an hour, I packed up and started to make my way back home, so happy that I decided to spend that early hour at the beach.

Throughout the day, I couldn't stop blushing, and his words stuck with me even throughout the night. Malik was so charming, but for some reason, there was something oddly special about him that I wanted to explore.

Every time I closed my eyes, I replayed his words over and over again in my head, like a scratched vinyl taking me back to that moment of vulnerability. I relished how he made me feel at that moment as I lay in bed and couldn't help but wonder if this was the start of something special and the beginning of a new chapter in my life.

***

Malik invited me out to dinner, and I didn't know what to wear, so I rummaged through my closet for the perfect outfit. Finally, I chose a white corset top and white high-waisted bootcut pants, which I paired with strappy open-toe sandals. I pulled my hair back in a sleek ponytail and chose my gold bangles and diamond studs passed down to me from my grandmother.

I was filled with excitement when the car arrived to pick me up, knowing I was about to see Malik again. The driver in his black suit opened the door, and all I felt at that moment was excitement and confidence—enough to make me feel like a queen.

There were couples seated throughout the five-star restaurant, and the ambiance of the lightly dim restaurant was romantic. When I entered, Malik rose from the table and greeted me with a hug and a kiss on the cheek. I was so nervous that the butterflies in my stomach were doing somersaults.

"You look stunning," Malik said.

"Thank you. You don't look too bad yourself."

Malik's black suit and white shirt with no tie provided a strong look of sophistication, more like a Barack Obama vibe. I felt as if I had taken on the role of Michelle. And from the looks of it, everyone in the restaurant thought so, too. They stared and smiled at us as if they were mesmerized by our strong, Obama-esque energy. Even more, we looked like a power couple that you'd see graced on the cover of *Ebony*.

As we waited for our dinner, the conversation between us flowed. I was irresistibly drawn to his magnetic charm. Our conversation danced between flirtation and intellect, his deep baritone voice resonating with each word. We talked about everything under the sun, and occasionally, we would burst into laughter. Though at times, I found myself fidgeting and I placed my hands beneath the table so that he wouldn't see my uneasiness.

"What made you move to Costa Rica?"

"I wanted a new scenery. Everything in my life was centered around work and no play."

"Were you seeing anyone?"

"I went on a few dates now and then, but nothing serious. How about you?"

"I was engaged to my college sweetheart, and we lived together. After two years of engagement, we started drifting apart."

"Do you guys keep in touch?"

"I usually hear from her around the holidays. She sends me a Christmas card in the mail. That's the extent of our communication."

"Do you still have feelings for her?"

"No, it's been a few years since we broke up, and I'm over her. I haven't had a serious relationship since then, but I have had a few situationships."

Oh, so he's one of those guys who likes to have his cake and eat it, too. I knew this was too good to be true. "Situationship is a clever way of being in a commitment-free relationship," I said, and judging by his expression, he saw the disappointment I was sure was written all over my face.

"I didn't mean it in a negative way. I've just had a few experiences where I wasn't ready for a serious commitment but still wanted a connection with someone. I can assure you that at this present moment, I am not dating to pass the time. I'm ready to settle down and possibly get married and have children. I want to be with that special someone," he admitted and smiled. "I've been focused on my business and making sure my parents are comfortable, but it's time to focus more on my future."

"Where do your parents live?"

"Here, and they love Costa Rica. They feel right at home. My parents are Panamanian. My dad was stationed here when he was in the military."

We had a lively conversation about our favorite books, movies, music, and even our dreams for the future. We shared stories from our childhoods, as well as our thoughts on current world events. I was stunned by his fluency in Spanish and impressed by how he ordered our meal in Spanish.

We talked for what felt like hours before the waiter brought our meals to the table, interrupting our flow. The conversation quickly shifted back to mundane topics, but the connection between us was undeniable.

Malik and I walked hand in hand down the beach after dinner, our laughter ringing out into the wee hours of the morning. The breeze strengthened and he draped his suit jacket over my shoulders protectively. When we said our goodbyes, he leaned in and kissed me. I went to bed that night, dreaming of us being together.

In the weeks that followed, Malik and I spent every waking hour together even though we had not consummated the relationship, and abstaining was becoming increasingly difficult. I was both excited and scared of the possibilities a future with him might hold.

Eventually, I decided that I was ready to take the next step in our relationship. I called him, and we made plans to meet to talk further about it, but an unexpected tropical storm hit, delaying that conversation.

The storm battered the region as heavy rain and wind pummeled the area, leaving many households without power. Thankfully, the generator sprang into action to restore service at the villa.

I heard a knock at my door, and there stood Malik in my doorway soaking wet. I quickly handed him a towel, and he removed his clothes. Before I could take everything to the machine to wash, he lifted me off my feet, bracing me against the wall and began kissing me passionately. He removed my sundress and began sucking on my breasts like he was in a candy store. He traveled downward and began sucking my vagina.

"Oh, Malik," I moaned.

"Oh, baby."

"Oh shit."

"Damn, baby."

The feeling of him inside me was like nothing I had ever experienced before. My inner walls swelled with desire as our bodies became one.

I pleasured him while he leaned back on the couch and allowed me to comfort him. He grasped my hips and moved my waist-length box braids to the side as he turned me over, and with my face down and ass up, he began thrusting his curved penis inside me.

As we reached a climax, our bodies shivered. We both rose up slowly as if the intimate tension between us had finally been relieved.

Afterward, we stepped in the shower together, allowing the warm water to cascade down our bodies as we shared a passionate moment of love.

***

We spent the remainder of the evening lounging on my sprawling sectional sofa, surrounded by a sea of plush pillows and cozy blankets.

I shared with him an album of my photography, and he studied the images closely as he expressed his admiration. "These photos are dope. You're so talented."

Grateful for his compliments, I responded with modesty, "Thank you. It's just a hobby of mine."

Half a bottle later, we became deeply invested in watching *Message in a Bottle*, starring Kevin Costner and Robin Wright Penn. The wine glasses, a partially lit scented candle, and a bowl of popcorn rested on the table next to us. When the movie ended, I was surrounded by the sounds of the rain pattering against the trees and snoring from Maverick, who curled in between us.

Throughout the night, I saw the same excitement and hope in Malik's eyes that I felt in my heart.

Eventually, we fell asleep, and each time I shifted, his embrace only grew stronger and more secure. I felt so safe in his arms that I didn't want him to let go. I knew then I had made the right decision. I was ready to take on the journey that lay ahead.

Chapter 3

Why Do Fools Fall in Love

Roxanne looked around the villa in awe. "This place is so beautiful!" The rest of my college crew agreed.

"What have we here?" Elena asked, her nose twitching with the delicious smells coming from the stove.

Elena looked a lot thinner since I saw her at Homecoming last year. Her gaunt face seemed to have been overshadowed by her boxed braids.

"I see you've been heavy on the pilates. You've lost a few pounds ."

"Yes, I'm trying to eat healthier."

I opened each of the pots on the stove to show off the dishes I'd prepared. The aromas wafted out and filled the entire house.

"I made some Casado. It's a Costa Rican dish made of beef stewed in red sauce with white rice, black beans, steamed vegetables and plantains.

"Tiff, that smells so good," Hannah cooed.

"Thank you, guys."

"Got a man and don't know what the hell to do with her damn self," Roxanne teased with a hand on her hip. We all started laughing.

"Don't be jealous." I grinned and winked at the girls.

I showed them their rooms, located directly across from each other at the rear of the villa. "This is where you'll be staying."

Everyone was on high alert with Maverick since the Mr. Feel Good incident. He couldn't contain himself knowing we had company, so he made numerous attempts to get the girls' attention, but they ignored him. A few times, they swatted at him, and Maverick took that as a cue to play.

"Tiff, please call Maverick," Roxanne begged as she began unpacking her clothes. "Yes, I'm talking about you," she added, speaking to Maverick directly.

Hannah said, "He's getting into everything. Can you keep him in a cage or something?"

"No, he doesn't stay in a cage."

Elena huffed. "Please call him."

"Come, Maverick. Come to Mommy," I said in a playful voice, and he came running at full speed.

I didn't want him to feel left out so I gave him a treat and kept rubbing his belly while we rolled together on the floor.

The girls were relieved when they heard Malik was taking Maverick home with him for the night.

Elena exclaimed, "Oh, that's a relief. If Maverick chews on my new shoes during this trip, his mama will have to compensate me for the damage."

I shouted from the bathroom, "I heard you," and we all burst out in laughter.

***

As we prepared to hit the town with Malik and his friends, the atmosphere in the villa was like a scene taken from our old college days in the dorm. Music from the mid-nineties filled the air as we ironed our clothing, laid out our outfits, and got ready to go. A few times, we broke out into a dance and sang along with the tunes playing in the background.

"That's my song," one of us would scream, and then a story would ensue.

We were walking around in our bras and panties and hair neatly tucked into bonnets and scarves. The bathroom counter was littered with all types of heat styling tools and every cosmetic brand on the market, lash glue included.

Tonight is going to be epic.

As I was getting dressed in my room, I thought about Malik, and I held my pillow. I was hypnotized by the aroma of his cologne that lingered on my sheets. Though we had been together just the night before, I already longed for his company, but I also felt a sense of confidence without him.

I was lost in thought when a sudden tap at my bedroom door diverted my attention. "Come in."

"Hey, do you have some bobby pins?" Roxanne asked.

"For what?"

"Girl, I need to secure this wig on my head with more bobby pins."

Roxanne donned a striking black bob wig that accentuated her gorgeous looks and her royal blue ensemble. As a senior auditor for Price Cooper Waterhouse and the resident comedian of our squad, she constantly kept everyone in good spirits with her wit and humor.

"Baby, I get to moving on the dance floor," Roxanne said in her thick New Orleans accent, "and this shit falls off my head, I'll have everyone scrambling for cover, thinking I'm there to rob the place with my cornrows and stocking cap on." We bellowed in laughter until Roxanne sobered and gave me a puzzled look. "What's wrong?"

"Nothing."

"You sure?"

"I was just thinking about Malik," I replied with a smile I couldn't hide.

"Girl, what?"

"I know you have a hard time keeping secrets, but I think I might be falling in love with him."

"Hmm, and only a few months in. Are you sure it's not just good sex?"

I laughed. "That's part of it, but my heart is in it too."

"Sounds like you're really invested. Who reacts first when you see him, your heart or your pussy?" she teased.

"I think it's a tie."

"We could talk about this all day. Sounds like you are feeling him."

"Yes, I do. I've never felt this way about anyone I've dated before." Roxanne looked up at me as though I had forgotten about someone, and I did. "Okay, maybe my ex, Langston, but this one feels right."

I spotted my cell phone on my bed next to a few pieces of jewelry, and my anxiety spiked when I noticed the time. The driver would be en route by then.

"Let me hurry up and finish getting dressed. The car will be here in a few minutes.

Roxanne nodded. "We'll finish this conversation later."

I was looking forward to introducing Malik to my friends, although they hadn't yet questioned me about him much, despite me talking about him quite a bit. I was confident they would let me know what they thought about him before the night's end and hoped it would be positive.

Malik had completely fulfilled my hopes and expectations for a partner, and I believed he was someone I could truly rely on. Our relationship was strong and unshakeable, something I had never experienced before with any man. He made me feel complete and whole, and I was confident I could trust him with my heart.

* * *

"Ladies, the car is here," I shouted from the front door as I waved down the driver, who almost passed the address.

We all strutted toward the car while supporting one another and taking care not to snag our high heels on the cobblestone driveway. As the driver held the door for us, I glanced at each of my friends and commented on how we looked like we were on our way to do a full-spread photo shoot for *Essence*. I wore a form-fitted black mini dress with my booty poppin', and I couldn't wait for Malik to see me in it.

As we pulled up, pulsating reggae beats reverberated from the club. The scene before us was a sight to see—dozens of women wearing clothes a few sizes too small, adorned with dazzlingly colorful wigs, and men carrying their drinks and joining in the festivities. The front of the nightclub was emblazoned with the Panamanian flag, proudly proclaiming the venue's heritage.

As the car came to a stop, Malik arrived and offered his help by gently taking our hands to help us exit the car. He gave me a huge hug and kissed me on the lips.

"Honey, these are my best friends, Roxanne, Hannah and Elena," I said.

"Hi, Malik," they all said in unison with huge smiles on their faces.

Malik greeted them in turn and gave his own introductions. "This is my cousin Mike, and my colleague and the VP of my company, Todd, and my classmate Guy."

While Malik's attention was elsewhere, Roxanne and the girls silently signaled their approval, and I responded with a grin.

Malik held my hand as we entered the nightclub, which was almost at full capacity. The club-goers spoke a mix of Spanish and

Jamaican patois, and the scent of white rum on the breaths of some of the men passing by pulled us forward.

Sitting at our table, Malik requested bottle service for our group. Once our drinks arrived, the eight of us sipped on our drinks and soon took to the crowded dance floor, swaying to the beats of classic reggae from the likes of Beres Hammond, John Holt, Dennis Brown, Buju Banton, Beniman and more.

Malik and I were so into the music that our bodies moved as one to the vibrant rhythm of the beat, as did the couples around us who were practically simulating sex acts.

Malik's deep roots in the Jamaican culture were on full display as he immersed himself in his favorite reggae music. His grandparents had migrated from Jamaica to Panama to work on the Panama Canal, and their cultural influence had clearly rubbed off on him.

We danced all night and made out on the dance floor like teenage lovers. A few times, I looked over to see Roxanne and Guy getting busy on the dance floor and so were Hannah and Mike, who immediately made a connection.

Elena and Todd talked most of the night at the table. She danced to a couple of songs but appeared tired and not herself. I suspected she was longing for her husband Greg, who she had been dating since college. Out of the four of us, she was the only one who had maintained a successful, long-term, committed relationship.

At one point in the evening, Malik and I skirted our way across the dance floor, arriving at the opposite end of the nightclub. The dim lighting obscured most of our surroundings, with only the aqua-blue walls, bar lights, and the occasional glimpse of the kitchen door providing illumination.

As we made our way behind the DJ's booth, towering speakers caught our attention. Each of them had a height and width of six feet. The DJ remained out of sight from the bustling dance floor.

We went behind those speakers, and Malik sat on a velour-covered bench attached to a wall. He leaned back against the wall with his eyes closed as I sucked on his hard penis. The rawness of it made me wet and steamy inside. I then made my way up to his lap and straddled him as he pulled up my dress and began sucking on my D-cup breasts. I glanced to both sides, checking to see if anyone was watching, even though, by then, it was too late to worry about it. I saw no one, not even the DJ.

Malik penetrated me and thrust inside as I bounced in his lap. While the pulsating reggae beat blared from the speakers, the sex was so intense that I momentarily forgot about the crowded nightclub, and any worries about being caught vanished.

Malik held me tight against him as my inner walls began to contract and clasp his penis like a fitted glove. Beads of sweat trickled down his forehead as his body jerked upward as he climaxed and called out my name.

He took a deep breath, trying to regain his composure from the intense physical exertion. He looked around while adjusting his belt, and I quickly straightened my bra and red g-string as he zipped up the back of my form-fitting dress. Then, we quickly made our way back to the table, where the drinks kept flowing.

***

Once we arrived home, my friends headed to their rooms and crashed while Maverick excitedly came toward Malik and me, eagerly wanting to go for a walk, so the three of us took a calming stroll along the shoreline.

Malik was visibly exhausted. His eyes were bloodshot—probably due to all the white rum and dancing—his lids half-closed. Still, I mustered up the courage to start a conversation about our relationship.

Before I could even finish my sentence, Malik locked eyes with me and said, "I love you, Tiffany."

"I love you, too," I quickly replied.

"Baby, you have brought so much happiness to my life. I haven't felt this way in a long time. When I'm not around you, I can't keep still, wondering if you're thinking about me. When I see you, I feel like the luckiest man on this planet."

His words left me in tears as I shared that no man had ever treated me this way. I assured him that my love for him was just as strong.

"Are you sure?" he asked with a sense of uncertainty in his voice that I'd never heard before. I assured him I was, and he leaned in and kissed me.

We watched the stunning sunrise as we held each other close, eventually drifting off to sleep while wrapped in each other's embrace. Sometime later, the bright sun woke me, and I quickly realized that Maverick was no longer by our side.

"Malik, baby, wake up. Maverick ran off. Please, can you help me find him?"

"Maverick," Malik yelled as he rubbed his eyes.

We ran along the beach and couldn't find him anywhere.

"Oh, I hope he didn't run out to the main road. Maverick, come, baby! I called out over and over again.

And just as panic began to set in, Maverick came rushing toward us from the shrubbery, energetically wagging his tail in excitement and causing both Malik and me to stumble to the ground unintentionally, laughing and relieved.

***

As I entered my bedroom, I heard the sound of rushing water running from my bathroom, and there was Elena bent over the toilet.

"I'm sorry. I didn't want to wake the others up, so I came in here." She attempted to stand but collapsed back onto the floor.

"Oh my God, are you okay? Do you want me to take you to the hospital?

"No, I'm okay. I think I drank too much. I just want to lay down. Can you help me?"

"Of course. Let me prepare you some ginger tea."

"I'm not sure if it's going to stay down."

"Just try it, Elena, and see what happens."

After tucking her in, I offered her a comforting cup of ginger tea infused with coconut milk and sweetened with honey to calm her unsettled stomach. When I returned from taking a shower, Elena had dozed off to sleep.

Chapter 4

Love Jones

The following evening, comfortably dressed in our pajamas, my girls and I listened to music and enjoyed a glass of wine while reminiscing about our night out with Malik and his friends.

I had on a red and white onesie with Mickey Mouse on it, along with my eyeglasses, and had my hair up in a messy bun. Next to me was Elena, wearing a red and white striped onesie complete with a hair bonnet, while Hannah wore blue pajamas. In contrast, Roxanne looked perfectly put-together in a long, black silk nightgown and robe and fur-covered slippers, with her curls remaining intact.

Elena inquired, "Where are you headed to? The Oscars?"

"Just to sleep," Roxanne replied.

Hannah quipped, "Alright, Diahann Carroll."

Roxanne rolled her eyes. "Not Diahann Carroll, just practicing self-love, bish. Don't be jealous because I prioritize my well-being." She turned to me and added, "I hope you're not wearing those overly worn Mickey Mouse pajamas to bed when you're with Malik."

"Malik actually loves my Mickey jammies. He thinks they're sexy." I stood and turned in a circle to show off my pajamas.

Roxanne shook her head in disapproval and took a sip of her wine. "I suppose some things remain the same," she muttered.

"Yep, Bish, some things never change," I responded, and we all laughed out loud.

Although it was obvious Malik and I were in love, I couldn't wait to tell my friends that we were officially a couple. And by the looks of it, I had a feeling there were some mutual interests or attractions between my friends and his.

"Yes, I gave Guy a kiss," Roxanne admitted. Everyone looked over at her with varying expressions of disbelief. "What? We were flirting all night," she added with a shrug. "He was feeling on my booty all night."

"Yeah, I saw you two on the dance floor," Elena threw in. "I was like, damn, go get a room."

Even Roxanne laughed at that. "We're going to keep in touch. He's always in Atlanta for business, so we exchanged cell numbers and email addresses."

I looked over at Hannah to get the scoop from her about Mike. "Hannah, you and Mike were rather close on the dance floor."

"He's a sweetheart. I really enjoyed his company, and we are definitely going to keep in touch. Look, guys, he sent me a text this morning. She shrieked in laughter and smiled from ear to ear.

"Well, it looks like we have a potential new couple in our midst," I cheered as the group's self-appointed matchmaker, then turned to Elena next. "What did you think of Todd?"

He's nice looking, but you know I would never cheat on Greg."

"Of course not," we all replied in unison.

Although Elena had been committed to Greg since their freshman year, she had ample opportunities to date other men. While she was trustworthy, we weren't always certain about Greg's fidelity, but we could never confirm our suspicions.

But Elena was happy with Greg. "I love him for who he is," she said with a smile. "Besides, I don't need any distractions right now. I'm focused on raising our two beautiful children and advancing my career goals."

We all nodded in agreement, knowing that Elena was a driven and hardworking person, and we respected her dedication to her children and career as a trial litigator for one of Atlanta's most prominent Black law firms.

I wanted so badly to change the conversation to Elena's sudden weight loss and her morning vomiting.

Earlier that day, Malik told me Todd insisted that Elena had nothing to drink last night. So, her claim of drinking too much was a lie. I encouraged her to take a pregnancy test, but she assured me she was not expecting. I can't imagine her keeping something serious from us.

Despite my worries about Elena's health, I gave her my word that I wouldn't mention anything about earlier that morning. As the only one among us capable of keeping a secret, I had to respect her boundaries.

Hannah, a local news anchor in Atlanta, was known as "CNN" back in college due to her knack for breaking news and always knowing the scoop behind every breakup on campus. Roxanne also struggled to keep things under wraps. But Elena had complete trust in me, knowing that I would never betray her.

"I just have to ask you all, what are your thoughts on my man?" I inquired, sitting up from my lounging position on the couch and studying their expressions.

"Girl, Malik is a catch," asserted Roxanne.

"It's obvious you two have a strong connection," Elena noted.

Hannah asked, "Are you two officially a couple?"

"Yes, we're together and head over heels for each other," I replied.

"Yasss! Black love in the house!" Roxanne cheered, giving us all a high-five.

As everyone started teasing and congratulating me, a warm feeling spread through my mind.

Maybe taking a chance on love wasn't such a bad idea after all.

***

Several weeks passed after my friends returned home, and I couldn't help but miss them dearly. I was back to my usual work routine, and Malik and I had grown even closer to the point where we were practically living together, and Maverick was our child.

Once we finished our dinner, the three of us set out for our evening stroll along the beach. It was our time to reflect on our day and check in with each other.

Malik asked, "Babe, is everything okay?"

I was surprised he noticed my troubled expression.

"You've been lost in thought since we left the house. Is everything good between us?"

I squeezed his hand. "Of course. I couldn't have asked for a better man than you."

"Then what's wrong?"

I took a deep breath before confessing, "I'm unhappy with my job. I'm bored as hell."

His eyes lit up. "What would you like to do?"

"I'm not sure."

"You love cooking and photography. Why not create your own content?"

My mind raced at the idea. "My own content?"

Malik smiled. "Sure. Why not start a cooking show? Talk to my sister for guidance."

Excitement filled me. "That's a great idea!" However, doubt quickly seeped in, making the idea feel unattainable.

He lifted my chin. "Babe, look at me. You can do this," he reassured me, wiping the tears from my eyes. "And I'll be here to support you every step of the way."

I spent several weeks anxiously planning and charting my first production shoot, choosing Malik's sister Rose as my director. I meticulously chose my debut meal: oxtails along with rice and peas, cabbage, and plantains—and with various clothing options in mind, I aimed for perfection.

Our filming stretched over the following week, covering ten segments, with Malik appearing in two. The process of video recording on an iPhone, an LED ring light with a tripod stand and later editing was pure joy. It felt as though I had finally discovered my true calling.

Together with Malik, I established a lifestyle website that highlighted my life in Costa Rica with recipes, blog articles and photos.

The anticipated go-live date was scheduled for the following month. My fingers were crossed, but I eagerly anticipated a positive response. I didn't know how to repay Malik, but I was determined to do something special for him in return.

***

I had a courier deliver an invitation to Malik's office.

Dear Malik,

I cordially invite you to join me for dinner at Chateau Tiffany at 7:00 PM. I have prepared a special meal for us that I am sure you will enjoy.

Please let me know if you have any preferences so that I may accommodate them accordingly.

I look forward to seeing you soon and having a wonderful evening together.

Love you,
Tiffany

Malik immediately texted me and accepted the invite, but desperately wanted to know what was for dessert. I told him that was for him to find out.

I greeted Malik at the door wearing a red lace thong negligee and black pumps with my hair pulled in a high ponytail.

I served dinner over candlelight while classic R&B love music played in the background. And when I placed the plate in front of him, his eyes opened wide with excitement as he saw I had prepared his favorite meal of steak, garlic mashed potatoes and asparagus.

I poured him a glass of wine, and he rubbed my ass before gently slapping it and whispering, "I can't wait for dessert.

We laughed throughout the entire meal as I struggled to find the right words to say to him in Spanish. I thought it would add to the ambiance if I spoke to him in Spanish, but I hadn't studied the language since high school, and my Spanish had not improved since living in Costa Rica.

May I have the pleasure of this dance, Tiffany Nicole Myers?" he politely requested.

"Absolutely," I happily accepted while extending my hands to him.

He led me to the center of the room and held me close as we slow danced to the sound of Jeffrey Osbourne's "Love Ballad." I rested my head on his chest and found comfort in the rhythm of his heartbeat.

Looking at me sensually, he spoke softly when he said, "Baby, thank you for this beautiful dinner. You remind me every day why I fell in love with you. No one has ever done anything special like this for me before. Thank you for showing me what real love is all about." He leaned in and kissed me tenderly on the lips.

Malik singing into my ear was as unpolished as my Spanish skills, but I thought it was a sexy gesture.

Later, when he expressed his desire for dessert, I went to the fridge and pulled out some whipped cream before blowing out the candles. I then led him to my bedroom, where we stayed until dawn.

Chapter 5

Lady Sings the Blues

While Malik and I slept soundly, his wallet, cell phone and an empty whipped cream bottle left on the nightstand accompanied my cell phone, which startled me awake with its vibrating alert.

I wasn't sure if I was in deep slumber or caught in a dream-like state. I bolted awake and snatched up my phone before it woke Malik as well.

A text message from Greg immediately caught my attention. It read, "Hey! Elena has been rushed to Emory Hospital, and it's serious."

I tried calling him, but it went straight to voicemail, and neither Hannah nor Roxanne were answering my frantic calls. I began searching for flights and was able to purchase a direct flight from San Jose to Atlanta, departing just a few hours later.

My heart raced as I scrambled out of bed and rummaged through my clothes. I needed to get to the airport as soon as possible.

I woke Malik and quickly filled him in on what had happened. He got dressed just as quickly as I did, and we rushed out the door with Maverick behind us.

Malik held my hand with his other on the steering wheel as we drove in silence to the airport. My mind whirled with questions.

What happened to Elena? Was she okay? Did her vomiting in my bathroom have anything to do with her illness? Why weren't Hannah and Roxanne answering their phones?

When we pulled up to the airport check-in, I kissed Malik goodbye and rushed to exit the car.

Once you're settled, give me a call," he shouted out of the window. "Sure. I will."

Upon reaching the sliding doors, Malik hollered, "I love you."

I turned and repeated the words to him, "I love you too." Then, Maverick began to bark, seemingly expressing his affection as well.

As tears streamed down my face, I realized this was the first time I would be apart from Malik since we began our relationship. I wanted to run back to the car and be with him—I missed him already—but I really needed to be there for my friend.

As the plane took off, I closed my eyes and sent silent prayers for Elena's well-being, hoping that the doctors would find a way to treat her condition and make her healthy again.

As soon as I landed, I received text messages from Hannah and Roxanne, saying they would meet me at the hospital.

When I arrived at the hospital, I rushed to the front desk and asked for Elena's room number. The receptionist directed me down the hall, and I ran toward her room.

As I approached, I heard the sounds of beeping machines. When I entered her room, my heart dropped. Elena was sleeping, and she looked so frail and pale, hooked up to all sorts of tubes. Greg sat next to her, tears in his eyes. Hannah and Roxanne gestured to me to sit next to them. They held my hand, and I didn't know what to do or say. All I could do was sit there and pray.

***

As we waited for the nurses to finish attending to Elena, the doctor came to the waiting room. As he approached us, we stood with an expression of desperation on our faces.

"The doctor inquired, "Who is Elena's next of kin?"

Without hesitation, we responded as a group, "We all are." Greg further clarified, "I'm Elena's husband and the father of her children, and these are her best friends."

"What's her prognosis? I asked.

The doctor's expression became solemn as he began to speak. "I'm afraid Elena's test results have revealed that she has colon cancer. We'll do everything we can to manage her symptoms and make her as comfortable as possible before she transitions."

We were all stunned by the news, tears beginning to fall down our faces as we realized the gravity of the situation.

We gathered around, held hands and commenced praying, begging God to heal Elena and acknowledging that, ultimately, He holds the power to make the final decision.

Mostly, we knew that we had to cherish every moment we had left with Elena and support her in any way that we could.

***

When Greg was finally able to bring Elena home, we waited inside, frozen in position.

"Surprise!" we shouted in unison. Elena's expression was one of utter shock. She looked around the room to see familiar faces from work, church and neighbors. Her children rushed toward her with presents in their hands.

Elena's weakened state didn't stop her from pulling her children in tight for a hug, tears streaming down her cheeks. It had been several weeks since she had been home. She had large square-framed black sunglasses on, and she wore a billowy white top paired with faded blue jeans and a vibrant head scarf with splashes of red, camouflaging the ravages of her illness and the intensive treatments that had already thinned her hair.

As soon as I saw Elena, memories of our initial encounter at Morris Brown College came flooding back.

The financial aid line snaked around the corner, but Elena and I kept ourselves entertained by chatting away about her Ohio roots, attractive guys on campus, our classes and aspirations for the future.

With her captivating beauty, she could put anyone at ease, but there was always more to her than meets the eye. We hit it off so well that we decided to become roommates.

The following day, we met up, and Elena helped me move into the dorm, where we were also introduced to Roxanne and Hanna, who lived on the same floor. The four of us quickly became friends and later roommates in an off-campus apartment, the infamous CC-4. Little did we know this encounter would foster a lifelong friendship.

While she was in the hospital, Elena's bedroom underwent a few changes to accommodate her needs. The girls and I worked tirelessly to rearrange every piece of furniture to ensure that Elena would be comfortable in her time of need.

I captured a few candid moments with my camera between the kids, Greg, Hannah, Roxanne, and myself. These photos were put up on the walls, complemented by balloons and flowers, to enliven the room's ambiance.

As the evening came to a close, Hannah and Roxanne stayed behind to assist with tidying up and getting the children ready for bed. Meanwhile, Greg, who has been working as a firefighter since graduating from college, grabbed some dinner before rushing off to work.

He entered their bedroom, where Elena was snuggled up under blankets. Dressed in his uniform, Greg wore a deep navy-blue T-shirt accented with the red emblem of the Dekalb County Fire Department. He also wore sturdy black boots and heavily reinforced cargo pants, complete with reflective stripes running down the sides.

"I love you, babe," he said.

She responded softly, "Bye, sweetie." He promised to call her later if she was still awake and kissed her on the lips.

"Bye, ladies," he then said, to which we all responded with our own goodbyes as well.

We laid across Elena's bed, reminiscent of our college days, and chatted about everything under the sun. Our conversation eventually turned to the secret we had all been keeping from each other about Elena's failing health.

As it turned out, I was not alone in sensing that something was amiss. Elena had a talent for making everyone feel like her closest ally. However, we were all tormented by the uncertainty over her condition. Nonetheless, she somehow managed to alleviate our worries and instill in us a sense of calmness, assuring us that things would turn out all right.

I was excited to show the girls a few select episodes from my cooking show on YouTube. Since Elena and I were the food lovers in our circle, she particularly showed a keen interest. I told them my plan was to launch the series in the fall.

Eventually, knowing that Hannah and Roxanne had to go to work in the morning, I had to log into a work meeting first thing the next day, and Elena had a packed day ahead of her with visits tomorrow from her yoga instructor, a nurse practitioner and nurse aides, we decided to call it a night.

Malik and I spent hours catching up on WhatsApp, discussing everything that had transpired since I left Costa Rica. I made sure to check on Elena and replenish her water throughout the night, even though I did doze off a couple of times.

At one point, Malik dozed off mid-conversation and started snoring, prompting me to suggest we continue our talk later in the day. Despite our fatigue, we continued chatting for several hours before finally succumbing to sleep.

After realizing the time, my focus shifted to preparing breakfast and ensuring the kids were dressed and out the door for school. Conveniently, their school bus arrived just outside the front door.

I prepared a nutrient-rich green smoothie for both Elena and myself. At exactly 8:00 AM, a nurse's aide arrived to assist Elena with daily tasks.

After I came back from my walk, Elena asked if I could retrieve her yoga mats that were stored in her upstairs closet. While scavenging for the mats, a plastic CVS bag surfaced. It contained pictures, loose coins, a half-empty value pack of Magnum condoms and an opened packet of Doublemint gum, all of which tumbled to the floor.

One of the photos inside was of Greg and a mystery woman, and they appeared to be romantically involved. Knowing better than to tell Elena, as it would surely devastate her, I cautiously placed the bag where I found it and took hold of the yoga mats.

I couldn't believe what I had just seen. Was Greg truly cheating on Elena? I couldn't believe this was happening.

***

One day, after tucking the children in bed, I peeked into Elena's room to see how she was doing. Although Elena had her fair share of good days, she also had days and nights where she appeared hopeless and remained silent, often staring out the window.

I was uncertain about whether I should give her some personal space or try to lift her spirits with amusing stories from our college days. In the past, that always seemed to work.

I longed to share with her what I had discovered, but I held back from doing so because I didn't want to cause her any more pain.

The sound from her TV could be heard from the hallway, with Hannah's signature voice leading the news broadcast. Once I stepped inside, I caught the tail end of the news broadcast, with Hannah and her co-anchor sending goodbyes to their audience just before a *Late Night with Jimmy Kimmel* commercial came on.

I noticed how Elena's hair had begun to grow back after finishing chemo, giving her the appearance of a buzz cut. Her skin had also regained its reddish-brown mahogany hue, emphasizing her defined facial features.

Standing at five-foot-ten-inches with a slim figure, she exuded a model-like appearance. Her high cheekbones protruded elegantly, overshadowing her somber round eyes. Despite Elena's illness, her natural beauty shone through even brighter.

"Come sit down," Elena said.

As her phone started ringing, I navigated my path toward her huge recliner chair. "It's Hannah calling," Elena announced. "She just left the news station."

It wasn't anything new to hear from Hannah at this hour. She typically yearned for someone to keep her company while she commuted back home to Snellville.

Lately, Elena had been Hannah's confidante when it came to her workday struggles and various office rumors. Despite being the highest-paid woman news anchor in Georgia, she was still subjected to discriminatory micro-aggressions.

Elena answered the call and put it on speaker. "Hey, Elena, how are you feeling?"

"I'm doing alright. I'm here with Tiffany. I was experiencing some joint pain earlier. Thankfully, the medicine I took after dinner relieved it."

Hannah said, "Weed can do wonders for that. I could use some my damn self. Those folks in the newsroom could drive anyone to light up."

"Well, you know we're talking about medicinal cannabis here," I threw in with a laugh.

"Same thing," Hannah exclaimed. "The news director is really getting on my nerves. Did you know his wife asked him for a divorce? I don't blame her ass. I would, too, if I had to share space with that fool."

Elena and I nodded in agreement. "Yes, you've told us before," I said.

Before she could go any further, Elena thankfully changed the subject. "Ladies, I want to run an idea by you guys."

After getting the go-ahead from both Hannah and me, Elena said, "Well, I want to start recording messages to Kniyah and Greg Junior. I'm concerned that they'll forget who I am if something were to happen to me."

Elena's voice trailed off as she looked at me, hoping that I would understand her concern. I nodded in agreement, as I did understand.

Elena continued. "I thought about making videos or writing letters, something they can watch or read when they get older. I want them to remember not just what I look like but how I sound and how much I love them."

Hannah spoke up. "That's a great idea, Elena. We'll help you record the videos and write the letters. Anything you need. Your kids will know how much you love them no matter what happens."

Elena started crying. "I'm so relieved and grateful for having supportive friends like you guys. I know it won't be easy to talk about these things, but I have to plan for the future and ensure my children will always remember me.

Chapter 6

A Thin Line Between Love and Hate

Being around Greg made me uneasy, especially after discovering that he was cheating on Elena.

One day, while I was preparing a salad for her in the kitchen, he initiated a conversation with me. "How's the progress on the video diaries going?"

"So far, everything is going well. She did break down a few times, but we managed to get through a lot today."

He nodded. "Let me know if there's anything she needs."

"We're good for now, but I'll keep you posted."

For some reason, his demeanor made me suspect that he had more to say. Even though he occasionally checked in on Elena after returning from work, I expected him to spend more time with her, considering his wife was terminally ill. Their relationship didn't seem passionate in any way, but Elena didn't seem bothered by it.

Although he didn't converse with me and the girls much during college, many women adored him for the same reason Elena fell in love with Greg—his rich chocolate skin, good looks, high IQ, and the fact that he was a Marine. The only change to his physical appearance after the years that had passed since then was his salt-and-pepper goatee, and for some women, that was an added feature.

Even though Elena was considered one of the most attractive girls on campus, dating was never her priority. Her main focus was on achieving excellent grades in school, as she had her sights set on attending law school.

While Elena did not immediately fall in love with Greg when they first met, he was relentless in his pursuit of her. Greg would consistently surprise Elena, showing up at her classes with flowers and leaving handwritten notes under her dorm room door. This continued for about a year until, one day, Elena decided to give him a chance. Everyone, including Greg, was shocked by this unexpected change of heart.

As Greg and Elena's romance grew into a committed relationship, they became inseparable. Elena could hardly go anywhere without Greg by her side.

Initially, I viewed this as admirable, but later, I recognized it as a type of control. It became clear overtime that Greg felt somewhat intimidated by the strong bond Elena had with us. He desired a more exclusive connection with Elena, but she wasn't willing to give up her close relationships with her girls. Elena viewed her women friends as an important part of her life, considering them to be like family.

I could confirm that Hannah, Roxanne, and I never criticized each other's significant others. By keeping our dating lives private, we preserved our friendship through time.

***

During my birthday lunch, I confided with Roxanne and Hannah my suspicion of Greg cheating. Roxanne was shocked, and Hannah was visibly shaken, calling Greg a "bastard." She began to cry.

"His timing couldn't be worse. Elena is dying while he sneaks around with another bitch." Hannah sneered.

Roxane expressed her frustration with men in general, but I reminded them that we don't have actual proof and accusing him would be unfair.

However, Hannah pointed out, "Come on, Tiff. Empty condom packets and pictures with another woman are clear evidence of cheating. Roxanne concurred, calling Greg a cheater.

Despite this, I maintained that we should mind our business until we had concrete proof.

After much urging, Roxanne and Hannah finally agreed in the best interest of our best friend that we would wait until we had more evidence, and we moved on to a lighter topic. However, I couldn't shake off the feeling of unease that lingered inside me. I knew I had to be patient and gather more evidence before I could confront Greg, but it was a tough situation. Still, I was determined to do the right thing, no matter how uncomfortable it would be.

I confided in the girls about how disappointed I was that Malik hadn't made an effort to visit since I came to Atlanta. He knew how much my birthday meant to me, but he hadn't shown any concern.

While Elena was not present at the gathering due to the doctor's advice to avoid crowds, it was strange not having her at my birthday outing. Elena always led the charge in organizing our *Sistah* Summits, and if her absence was a glimpse into our future without her, it was going to be a tough road ahead for us.

In spite of everything, I felt a sense of gratitude for the time I had with Roxanne and Hannah. We reminisced about our old memories and talked about plans for future trips. It was a reminder of how important friends are, especially during tough times.

As we finished our meal, I couldn't shake the feeling that things were going to be different from now on. But with Roxanne and Hannah by my side, I knew we could get through anything together.

We spent most of my birthday at the spa, and they gifted me a hotel stay at the Hyatt Regency. Since Malik wasn't coming, I'd be spending it alone. Despite this, Hannah and Roxanne hinted at even more surprises to come, so we eagerly set off on our next adventure.

Everyone gathered around the island in Elena's kitchen, where a round cake with yellow and white frosting sat, bearing the name "Tiff" and adorned with a small number of candles in the center. As the group burst into song, the children shouted eagerly for the birthday girl to make a wish. I silently prayed that God would heal Elena.

As the adults raised their glasses in a toast, Elena expressed her gratitude for the time I'd been able to give her family. To my surprise, Greg also made a toast and thanked me for looking out for his children and Elena.

"You don't know how much it means to me to know that Elena has friends she can count on," Greg finished.

As he spoke, Hannah and Roxanne remained silent, and I could sense that Hannah was holding back from confronting him. Despite her desire to speak up, she kept her promise and refrained from saying anything. We were all behaving well and keeping our secret safe. As for Greg, he seemed to have no worries in sight.

Most of the night, we danced, and even Elena stepped into the middle of her living floor dancing like she did in college as a Bubbling Brown Sugar.

We ended the night doing the Soul Train Line, where I dropped on the floor and landed in a split. I thought to myself, *I am going to pay for this later*. The kids and Greg were in shock, and Hannah and the girls cheered me on. We were all in fits of laughter.

Roxanne occasionally excused herself to take phone calls. At one point in the evening, she returned with a sly whisper that she had an exciting date lined up and she was ready to go. It didn't surprise me she had a man waiting for her. Roxanne's ability to magnetize men was well documented.

She was a trailblazer before the advent of Meg Stallion. And despite gaining an additional thirty pounds since college, her hourglass figure still turned heads on Atlanta streets. From her college days, she always had suitors her age or older who lavishly spent money on her. Despite having been proposed to six times, she ended up breaking off every relationship.

As soon as we got into the car, she handed me a gift and urged me to open it. Eager with anticipation, I ripped off the wrapping paper like a child on Christmas morning. To my surprise, it was a stunning set of black lingerie with matching panties, complete with a lock and key.

"Thank you, Roxanne. I'll certainly have to showcase this to my man in Costa Rica."

"Yes. No more Mickey Mouse onesies," she said sarcastically.

"Whatever," I said with a dismissive wave, and we both bellowed in laughter.

As we arrived at the Hyatt Regency, elegantly attired couples were entering and exiting the hotel. I couldn't help but feel underdressed in my denim jeans and plain white top despite my exposed back. I had my hair down and had adorned myself with bold brass earrings loaned to me by Elena from her trip to Africa.

When I checked into the hotel, I received my key from the front desk agent and proceeded to head up to my room. My mind kept wandering back to Malik and how he had failed to reach out to me since earlier in the day, which left me feeling quite let down. But ultimately, I made a decision not to dwell on it and waste my birthday evening. Instead, I opted to indulge in a relaxing soak in the tub and adorn myself with some alluring lingerie.

I entered the card key and pushed the door handle down. My eyes were greeted with a mesmerizing sight—red rose petals and candles strewn all around, illuminating the room with a warm glow. And there he was, standing close to the bed covered in rose petals—my Malik.

Overwhelmed with emotion, I let out a scream and jumped into his arms. Tears streamed down my face as I expressed my amazement.

"I was sure you weren't coming," I cried.

"Sweetheart, I wouldn't miss your birthday for anything in the world." He hugged me tightly as I buried my head into his chest, feeling overwhelmed with emotions. This surprise visit was worth all the wait and anticipation.

He removed my top and bra, and he pulled off my panties and jeans. He began to pleasure me, sticking his tongue inside me and then sucking on my clit. I held onto the bed sheets for dear life.

He placed my legs over his shoulders. As he thrust inside me, he slowly gained momentum, causing my breasts to bounce. I held on to his muscular back as he sucked on my nipples and kissed me all over my neck and mouth.

"Malik," I screamed. "Oh God, this feels so good."

He turned me over and entered me from behind. We both came at the same time.

After our breathing regulated, we got up and ran into the Jacuzzi, where we fed each other chocolate-covered strawberries. We remained lost in the moment and the comfort of each other's arms for long minutes. Eventually, we went back to bed and drifted off to sleep, wrapped up in a blissful haze of pure excitement.

As the morning sun crept into the room, we woke up to a new day and made love again and again. We showered and hopped back in bed, where we spent most of the day ordering room service, laughing and talking.

Chapter 7

Eve's Bayou

People were starting to layer their clothing and bring out their winter gear as the Georgia weather began changing and the nights were getting colder. The leaves on the trees had turned shades of brown and gold, signaling the arrival of winter.

The drop in temperature had me yearning for Costa Rica even more, where I could bask in the sun and spend more quality time with Malik and Maverick.

My relationship with Malik remained the same. My heart still fluttered at the sight of him, and his eyes would light up when he saw me. However, I sensed that something was amiss. I couldn't pinpoint the problem, but I was unsure if I was attempting to sabotage our seemingly perfect relationship or if something was truly off.

I didn't know how to tell Malik how I was feeling. I loved him, and the last thing I wanted to do was to chase him off—something I habitually did in all of my romantic relationships.

I truly believed that our time apart was strengthening our bond. We made a deliberate effort to communicate regularly through WhatsApp and phone conversations, and I was confident that whatever feeling of uncertainty I was having would eventually go away.

***

While Elena's health was deteriorating, she maintained a hopeful outlook and dedicated herself to staying involved in her children's lives for as long as she could. Each morning, she pushed herself to rise early and fix breakfast and lunch for her kids, seeing them off to school before joining me on our walks.

During these quiet strolls, we usually held hands and listened to music or a sermon through our earbuds. Elena always played "I Hope You Dance" by Lee Ann Womack, her favorite song. Elena requested that it be performed at her funeral, which seemed fitting given her lifelong love of dance.

Elena dedicated a significant amount of time documenting her thoughts and experiences for her family, recording several messages for her children and husband. She even left a few recordings specifically for the girls and me. She had all the necessary equipment set up, with a tripod-mounted camera and a remote control to begin recording. She also had a ring light to help illuminate her and a microphone to capture her words clearly. At the end of the week, Jack, who worked as a production assistant at Hanna's news station, edited the footage. During these filming sessions, I made sure to give Elena her space as I knew how emotionally challenging it was for her.

Elena's condition was causing me great emotional strain. At times, I found myself furious with God. *How will I cope without her?*

I realized how self-centered my thoughts were and couldn't fathom what Greg and the children were going through, but I still couldn't help feeling the way I did. Elena was the voice of reason among our group of four.

My concern also extended to Hannah, who had started drinking a tad bit more than normal, adding to the struggles at work. Roxanne, on the other hand, seemed preoccupied with projecting an image of having everything in check. It was evident, however, that she, too, was hurting.

Elena called me into her room, grinning ear to ear. Immediately, I sensed that she had something planned.

"Hey, how about we all head up to the cabins in North Georgia? You, Greg, Malik, Hannah, Mike—everyone. We can make it a couples' retreat to celebrate our wedding anniversary. And I know Roxanne won't mind finding a date."

With her terminal illness weighing heavily on our minds, Elena knew that a getaway was just what we needed.

While I accompanied Greg and Elena on the drive to the cabins, Greg wasn't very talkative. He mainly focused on the GPS while Elena and I carried on most of the conversation until I dozed halfway through the journey.

Elena appeared to be in better spirits, playing music like Mary Mary's "Shackles (Praise You)." A few times, she checked in on the kids who were away with Greg's dad.

After traveling for almost five hours in Greg's Suburban, we finally arrived at the cabins. We were greeted by a stunning panoramic view of what seemed like all of Georgia. The cabins, resembling wooden mansions, were perched on the highest point of the mountain. The temperature had plummeted, creating a freezing atmosphere with an approaching snowstorm.

Hannah and Mike made their relationship official and headed out to one of the cabins together. Roxanne rode separately with her new man Scott, who we hadn't met yet—a Defensive End coach for the University of Georgia—who was also a single father of identical twin boys.

Another couple, who were friends with Greg and Elena, also planned to join us. His friend, Kevin, was an attorney who attended

Morehouse and Kevin's fiancée, a Spelmanite, was an ER physician who had been called into work but would arrive tomorrow. Unfortunately, Malik's flight was canceled, so his arrival was delayed, but he was expected to arrive later in the evening.

Greg and I took charge of settling Elena into the luxurious master bedroom suite on the bottom floor, to the far right of the kitchen. The personal chef, who was nearby, presented a vibrant charcuterie board adorned with cheeses, crackers, fruits, and vegetables and whipped up a pot of homemade chicken soup alongside an assortment of delectable sandwich wraps.

The snowfall intensified, and everyone promptly made it inside. By this time, Malik had notified me that he'd landed and the roads were liable to close soon, so he may need to lodge at the Hilton, located at the base of the mountain. I couldn't wait for his arrival. We had a lot of catching up to do since the last time we were together.

I made sure to pack some of his favorite lingerie bits and my Disney onesies for lounging. Meanwhile, I got settled into our room, which had a fireplace and a sliding door that led out to a balcony that had a jacuzzi. I changed into some comfortable clothing, excited to know I would soon see my man.

Both of us were disappointed, yearning to be together. My disappointment was evident to everyone, causing Greg's friend Kevin, who looked awfully familiar, to offer to accompany me to pick him up. But just as we were preparing to leave, Malik informed us that the roads were shut down with state troopers blocking entry points.

He said it was just too dangerous to take the risk of getting stranded in the snow but not to worry because the roads would be cleared by morning, and we would reunite before noon. We chatted for about an hour, and Malik finally relented to getting himself some food before room service ended.

I didn't want to be rude, so I joined the others as they played an exhilarating game of spades, and I kept myself busy by snapping photos of the couples. Heineken bottles and ashtrays filled the table with cigar smoke trailing upward. The couples were huddled together, with Roxanne fervently cheering her man on. Hannah and Mike teamed up in the game while the television blared with ESPN Sportscenter and nineties hits playing in the background.

Kevin's constant staring was making me uncomfortable. It was as if he knew me from somewhere, and I later realized he did. I nearly spilled my drink when it came to me, and he caught on, grinning like he could read my mind. The Omega tattoo on his shoulder was as conspicuous and enormous as I remembered, nearly taking up his entire shoulder. I got up and headed for Elena's room and bumped into Roxanne, who was coming out of the bathroom.

"What's wrong with you," Roxanne asked.

"Nothing."

Roxanne looked down at her watch and said, "Girl, Malik will be here in a few hours. Relax. You'll be okay."

I just rolled my eyes in disgust. "Is Elena awake?"

"She was up about half an hour ago."

I nodded and then knocked on the door.

"Come in," Elena shouted.

Elena was preparing for bed. She had her pajamas on and I noticed that her nightstand was equipped with a King James Bible along with a collection of medicine bottles.

"Hey, guys. What's up?" Turning to me, she added, "Did you get everything squared away with Malik?"

"Yes, he'll be here in the morning."

"Oh good." She smiled, and I could see on her face that she sensed something was off with me. "What's wrong?"

"Let's just say that I know Greg's friend Kevin quite well." I stood fidgeting like a child admitting that she had done something wrong.

"You had a class with him?" asked Elena.

"No."

With a perplexed expression, Roxanne furrowed her brows and narrowed her eyes as if she were onto something. "Oh shit. You fucked him. When? While we were in college or CC-4?"

"Damn, Tiff."

"Yes, like dozens of times."

Roxanne started pacing the floor as if she were coming up with a plan, and then she stopped midway. "Okay, that was a hundred years ago. Not a big deal. Atlanta is small, anyway. Hell, was the dick good? Speaking of good dick, let me get back to my boo with his fine ass. I'll holla at y'all later in the morning, maybe noon or whenever we decide to come up for air." She chuckled and swayed her hips as she exited the room.

Elena studied me. "That's no reason to be worried, Tiff."

"I know, but it's going to be awkward being around his fiancé and Malik."

"Well, I'm heading to bed now. See you in the morning, babe." She blew a kiss and requested that I turn off her lights.

When I returned to the living room, everyone had left. I couldn't sleep, so I decided to keep myself busy. I started washing the dishes, anticipating the chef's arrival in the morning to prepare breakfast. Suddenly, Kevin entered the kitchen looking casual in a Morehouse football alumni T-shirt and gray jogging pants.

I found myself drawn to him as he pulled a bottle of water from the fridge and offered to help me. "Hey, you need a hand with anything. I took a nap earlier this afternoon, and now, I can't sleep." He began collecting empty bottles around the room and storing them in a plastic bag.

"What's your name again?"

"Tiffany."

"Yeah, that's right."

Just then, Greg came in with his cell phone in his hand and told us good night.

While storing the food in the refrigerator, Kevin expressed he was craving some popcorn, and I had a taste for some, too, so, I prepared a bowl of popcorn for us, and then we sat on the couch.

He poured a glass of wine for both of us, and a brief, uncomfortable pause in the conversation followed as we both went quiet. He picked up the TV remote and started flipping through channels.

We both sat at opposite ends of the couch. I was curled up on my end with a blanket, and the fireplace crackled quietly in the background, casting a warm and cozy glow over the room. Despite the comfortable ambiance, the awkwardness between us was palpable as we both avoided eye contact.

We caught the tail end of an episode of Martin and found ourselves bursting with laughter, which helped ease the awkwardness between us.

"It's been quite a while, Tiff. How has life been treating you? I wasn't sure if you remembered me. When Greg invited my girl and me on this trip, he mentioned your name, but I didn't know it was you. By the way, you look fantastic. I mean, like, IG beautiful," he said. He looked me directly in my eyes and I felt squirmish.

"Thanks. I'm good. And how about yourself?"

"Things have been pretty hectic since I made partner at my law firm, but I'm doing great. This trip came at the perfect time. My girlfriend and I got engaged earlier this year."

"Congratulations."

"I heard you're living in Costa Rica now. That's incredible. I've always wanted to visit. How long have you and Malik been together?"

"About six months, but it feels much longer."

Kevin nodded. "It can be like that sometimes when you're having fun. My girl Maya and I have been together for two years.

It seems like we've been together for much longer." He paused before saying, "I'm struggling to find the right words to say to you. It may come across as unusual, but after the few times we hooked up, you never left my mind. I've often thought about you."

I laughed. "Are you sure about that? You couldn't remember my name."

"I remember everything else. You're head game," he said, chuckling with a smirk on his face. He brushed his hands across his crotch. "We had so much fun, Tiff. I also remember our late-night walks to grab something to eat. We would race each other back to my place."

"If you knew where I lived, why didn't you try to contact me?"

"I did a few times, but then I let my ego take over, and I moved on."

"You're in love?" I inquired.

"Yes, I am. But, when I saw you, Tiff, it brought back some great memories. We had a really, really good time," he emphasized.

I couldn't believe what I was hearing. But I had to admit his foolery caught my attention, and he was feeding me some bullshit. "Kevin, I have to be honest with you. I'm head over heels in love with Malik."

Kevin nodded. "He's a lucky man. But in case you have a change of heart, I'm here for you."

As my eyelids grew heavier, Kevin and I dozed off, only to be awakened by Malik and Kevin's fiancé early in the morning. Maya glared down at us, flipping her lace front the entire time. The ottoman held a bowl of popcorn, wine glasses, and a half-empty bottle of wine as Kevin and I stretched out on the couch. Sometime during the night, Kevin had managed to stretch himself out in my direction.

This was not what I wanted Malik to see. I quickly sat up and tried to brush off popcorn kernels from my pajamas. Kevin rubbed his eyes and yawned, oblivious to the tension in the room.

"Good morning," Maya said with a forced smile.

Startled awake by Malik, I smiled. "Hey, baby, you finally made it." He bent down and kissed me.

Maya seemed annoyed and glared at me with disgust. "Kev, I'm here. Wake up, baby."

"Okay, Tiff," Kevin murmured, still half asleep. Maya corrected him, reminding him that she was his fiancée.

After Kevin woke up startled, I introduced him to Malik, and they shook hands, but Maya refused to acknowledge me. Malik and I quickly walked away, and I directed him to our room.

***

Maya had Kevin under lock and key most of the following day, and on a few occasions, he walked past me without making eye contact.

That evening, Maya didn't utter a syllable even though during a few of the couples' games— Newlywed and Charades—Malik and I were paired up with them. Of course, we won. The competitor in me wasn't having it any other way.

Malik didn't suspect anything, and we carried on with our planned activities. The atmosphere was competitive but fun, and the room was consistently filled with Black excellence.

A few times, I looked over at Elena and could sense she wasn't feeling well. Her face appeared paler than usual, and her eyes were practically jaundiced.

"Babe, you want to lay down," Greg asked.

"No, I'm fine. I could use some water, though."

Malik jumped up and handed her a bottle of water from the fridge. She took a few sips of water and said, "I am going to head in. It's getting late." When she stood, she collapsed but landed in Greg's arms. Greg picked her up and carried her to the bedroom.

I couldn't help but feel sorry for my friend, who had an incessant fear of missing out on anything important.

Maya promptly sprang into action, retrieving her bag. "Greg, please allow me to check her vitals." The solemn expressions on everyone's faces were evident that the atmosphere had shifted dramatically.

As tears welled in Roxanne's eyes, Hannah lowered her head in sympathy, and Mike comforted her by gently rubbing her back. It was the first time I could remember Roxanne publicly displaying her emotions, and Scott was there to hold her close.

I placed my head on Malik's chest for support and comfort as we watched the scene unfold. We both knew how much Roxanne had been holding inside, and it was never easy to see someone you care about in pain. As we stood there quietly, giving Roxanne the space she needed to work through her feelings, I couldn't help but think about how lucky we were to have such a supportive group of friends. At that moment, I felt grateful for their presence and knew that together, we could get through anything.

A short time later, with a stethoscope around her neck and wearing a powder blue sweatshirt that read Spelman, Maya emerged from the bedroom and said, "Elena has a slight fever. I gave her some Tylenol, and she fell asleep. Greg is by her side. I also spoke to her doctor, and he wants to see her tomorrow morning. Hopefully, the roads will be cleared to allow for safe traveling."

Kevin hugged Maya as she shared Elena's progress, and everyone sighed in relief. We all started cleaning up. "You guys want to watch a movie," Kevin asked.

"No, we're heading to bed," Scott replied.

After I got out of the shower, I lay across the bed. It felt like the weight of the world had taken over my soul, and I was emotionally drained.

Malik got on top of me and began kissing me passionately. Before long, he was caressing my breasts, cupping my areola and sucking on my nipples as though he was keenly aware that his gentle touch was what I needed at that moment. He effectively alleviated any worries or uncertainties from my thoughts in no time.

He worked his way down to my inner thighs and then inserted his tongue in my vagina, where he moved it in and out and began sucking my clit.

I couldn't help but scream out his name and plead with him, "Please put it in now." And when he did, I threw my head back in sheer ecstasy.

Our bodies were magnetic—his penis rock hard entered me with a steady rhythm, and I became even more aroused. The way he touched me caused my emotions to overflow, and tears streamed down my face.

Concerned, he softly spoke, "Are you okay? Am I causing you pain?"

"No, baby." I smiled.

Gently wiping away my tears of joy, he continued making love to me. In a whisper, he expressed his love for me, and I reciprocated those feelings. As our bodies interwove like a human pretzel, we reached our climaxes in unison.

Malik then rested his glistening body upon mine, damp with beads of sweat.

I knew without a doubt that I wanted Malik to be a part of my life forever. He fulfilled every criterion on my checklist and more.

***

Malik was fast asleep, but my mind reverted back to Elena's well-being, making it difficult for me to rest. I tiptoed out of the room and went toward the kitchen for a glass of water.

To my surprise, I encountered a shirtless Greg in Dekalb County Fire Department emblem jogging pants. Our unexpected meeting startled both of us, causing us to jump in surprise.

Greg quickly apologized. "I'm sorry. I thought everyone was asleep."

"It's okay. How's Elena doing?"

"She's sleeping," he replied, looking like he had been crying.

Uncertain of what to do, I was relieved when Scott appeared, and soon, Hannah and Kevin joined us. We sat around the table and talked.

"Thank you for coming here with us," Greg began. "Elena was determined to celebrate our anniversary with everyone here, which means a lot to us. The thought of losing Elena is unbearable for me and my family." His voice trembled as he shared his concerns.

Scott reached out and squeezed Greg's hand. "Frat, stay strong. The final decision is in God's hands."

Greg agreed, stating that Elena had been reminding him of that as well.

"Would it be okay if we said a prayer?" asked Mike. We came together in a circle, holding hands and bowing our heads. "In Jesus' name, we humbly pray. Amen," we said before wrapping Greg in a group hug. Seeing him display vulnerability for the first time, I had no doubt he loved Elena.

As everyone prepared to depart the next day and get back to their daily routines, Elena presented each of us with parting gifts and a personalized note from her before saying goodbye. We exchanged hugs and vowed to reunite soon. Even Maya and I shared an embrace, and we promised to meet up for lunch.

Malik and I and Greg and Elena were the last couples to remain until the end. Malik helped Greg load the suitcases into the SUV, and since Malik had extended his trip a few extra days, he and I rode back together with Anita Baker's greatest hits playing in rotation.

Greg later reached out to everyone in a group text to say that Elena was hospitalized and that he would keep us posted.

Chapter 8

Above the Rim

Elena was finally released from the hospital. Her CT scans showed that the cancer was responding to the treatment. Despite our initial joy, we remained vigilant and prayed fervently for a miracle, as she was still facing uncertainty. The incident at the cabin and her extended stay at the hospital served as a reminder that we were all relying on hope and faith.

I traveled to Costa Rica multiple times since then, as there was a new administration in place, and Malik aimed to impress the council. I wanted to be there to support him.

We were overjoyed when his contract was extended by a unanimous decision for an additional five years. His work was receiving global recognition, and I couldn't have been prouder.

Despite an offer for a permanent remote position from the company that acquired my old job, I opted to continue to work as a contractor instead. I relished my independence and desired to unshackle myself from any one particular company.

I was back in Atlanta, and Elena seemed to be feeling better. She kept herself busy handling her business affairs and filming her diary. It took a lot of energy out of her, and she usually went to bed early but tried her best to see the kids before they went to bed and again before they left for school in the morning.

This one evening, after putting the kids to bed, I was standing at the bottom of the stairs when I overheard a conversation between Greg and someone on the phone. I heard him say, "I love you, too," before ending the call.

I didn't know what to do, and I waited for about thirty seconds before entering the room. When I did enter, he was startled. My mind raced, but I didn't want the tension to escalate, so I gathered the courage and confronted him.

"Greg, are you cheating on Elena?"

His body language gave him away; he averted his eyes and headed toward the window with his back turned to me. "I was talking to my son's mother." Did I just hear him right? Did he say his son's mother? Not Elena? This was getting worse by the minute.

"A few years ago, I met this woman named Camille at my kid's school, and we immediately clicked. We were friends before anything happened between us."

"Wait. I'm confused. During the cabin trip, you talked about how much you loved Elena and how you couldn't live without her."

"I wasn't lying."

"Have you talked to her about this woman?"

"Yes, I know about the affair," Elena announced from behind us.

We were shocked to see her awake and up, walking around, and especially startled to realize she had overheard our conversation.

Elena was aware of the infidelity, and to avoid further fallout, she asked us to sit down and discuss it calmly.

The doorbell rang, and I immediately jumped up from the couch to answer. I needed an excuse to step away for a moment to gather my thoughts.

I said, "It's Hannah and Roxanne. We were planning to grab a bite to eat. Do you want to talk about this later between the three of us?"

Elena shook her head. "No, they're eventually going to find out." She gestured to Greg to sit down, and moments later, Hannah and Roxanne walked in, both in a jovial mood with smiles on their faces.

Roxanne was clad in a Willi Smith purple vintage cashmere faux wrap long-sleeved blouse with some fitted denim blue jeans, gray thigh-high boots, and her LV purse. Hannah had her news anchor look on, which was her hair blown out, extra TV makeup, a suit jacket and slacks. I'm happy we weren't going anywhere. Apparently, I didn't get the memo. Same shit they used to do to me in college. I was wearing sweatpants and a sweater top two sizes too small that Elena loaned me.

Hannah and Roxanne noticed the somber mood, and I could see by their faces that they were beginning to worry.

"Is everything alright?" Roxanne asked.

Elena replied, "Yes, and I'm happy you guys are here. Please take a seat. I've been wanting to share something with you all."

I looked over at Greg to see if he was going to be man enough to lead the conversation and not have Elena clean it up for him. Elena began talking, and Greg interrupted her.

"I've been seeing another woman."

Hannah gasped. "How could you, Greg?" Roxanne shook her head in disbelief.

"I never intended on hurting Elena. I never wanted to do that."

"No, you just couldn't control your dick," Hannah said angrily.

"Hannah, please stop and let him finish," Elena said.

Greg stood and paced the room. His deep, dark skin glistened from the sweat beads that formed above his brow, but his feet were ashy and looked like he had stepped into a bowl of flour.

He seemed nervous and began biting his lip. "This woman gave birth to my son."

Hannah jumped up from the chair. "Oh, hell no. Elena, you're not condoning this shit, are you?"

"I was angry when he told me, and I'm still reeling over the pain."

"How old is this son?" Roxanne asked.

"He turns three in November."

"Wait a minute. So, this affair took place before she became sick?" I asked.

Elena said, "We were on a break from the marriage, and things weren't going so well with us."

"That doesn't give him a pass to step out on your marriage," Roxanne insisted.

Elena raised her head. "I've met the woman and think she would make a great mother to my children."

We all looked over at Elena as though she had lost her damn mind. "You can't be serious?" I asked her.

"Yes, I am serious. I'm dying, and I want to get to know this woman. I want to be sure she'll take good care of my children." Tears flowed from Elena's eyes.

Roxanne questioned her. "You've met her?"

"Yes. She's already met the children, and they've met their half-brother. She's great with them."

Hannah, on the other hand, had a different opinion. "Is there some sister-wife situation happening here that we don't know about?"

"No, not at all. She's a white woman and a few years younger than us."

"Wait. She's white?" Hannah and Roxanne exclaimed in unison.

Roxanne said, "Look, Elena, a woman who sleeps with a married man has a character flaw that you should be concerned about. Frankly, that's not someone you should want around your kids. Did Greg put you up to this?"

Greg denied being involved. "No, not at all. But Elena insisted on meeting her."

Elena pleaded for our support. "I want you guys to support me on this decision. I love my children, and I want to make sure that when I am not around, they'll be taken care of by a woman who loves my husband."

I said, "Hannah, Roxanne, and I will take good care of your children. As long as I'm breathing, your children will never go without." Turning to Greg, I asked, "Greg, do you see a future with her?"

He hesitated, looked over at Elena and looked down before saying, "I do."

Elena began crying, and we all comforted her.

I had my doubts, but I had to honor my friend's wishes. Hannah, on the other hand, was suspicious of Greg and Camille. The fact that Camille was white and younger only added to her suspicion. It was all triggering for her.

Hannah had financially supported her ex-husband through law school, only to be left for his much younger white law clerk when he became a federal judge. For months, she kept saying, "I was the only bitch who gave him the time of day when he was broke as hell."

Hannah suspected they wanted to cash in on Elena's life insurance money and run off into the sunset, so she hired not one but two private investigators. Camille's background check came back squeaky clean—not even a parking ticket came up.

Elena avoided talking badly about Greg in front of the kids. Camille began visiting the house frequently, and though the kids called her "auntie," they referred to her child as their brother.

The kids were too young to understand what was really happening. Elena began showing her how to make the kids' favorite meals, including her specialty, oatmeal sweetened with condensed and coconut milk, with almond butter and spices.

Their relationship began blossoming, but it was a gradual process. For obvious reasons, there was no trust there on either side. The one thing they did have in common was that they both loved the same man.

Occasionally, when I came in from my morning walks, Camille and Elena were deeply engaged in conversation. Meanwhile, I interacted with Camille as little as possible and maintained my distance.

I empathized with my friend's plight since she would go to any length to secure the best interest of her children, even if it meant suppressing her own feelings. I couldn't judge her. If this woman was going to be around her children, Elena wanted to at least know what she was all about. Like, did she have the temperament to raise children?

Camille seemed sincere, but I couldn't ignore the fact that she knowingly slept with my best friend's husband. I didn't trust her. Hannah wanted no part of her, and Roxanne just went along with everything for Elena's sake.

I was preparing lunch one day when Elena walked into the kitchen. You could tell she had a lot on her mind. She was sporting a fitted white top with denim capris and an eye-catching red and yellow scarf that pulled together in a donut-shaped circle formed in the center of her forehead. Despite her slim, five-foot-ten-inch frame that exuded a runway model, her demeanor made it clear that she was seriously ill and had limited time.

I offered her chamomile tea with agave honey while I prepared her favorite dish of lemon honey glazed salmon atop wild rice and roasted asparagus. Though Elena and I shared a love for good food, she was the more health-conscious one of the two of us. I loved and couldn't resist eating my favorite: lemon pepper wings with extra ranch dressing from Wingstop.

She carefully sipped on the tea while she opened up about Greg and Camille's affair. "I've known about Greg's infidelity for a while now, but we had been dealing with it privately.

"Honestly, I was too embarrassed to tell anyone. I thought we could work it out, but he fell short on his end of the deal and continued to see her. I was angry as hell, and then, to top it off, he had a child with this woman. I threatened to leave with the kids, but I really wanted to kill his ass. He begged me not to leave, so I stayed for my children."

Elena paused before continuing. "His explanation was that she gave him the attention he had been wanting for so long. Can you believe that shit? Was I not enough for him? Am I less deserving? I mean, come on, Greg."

I said, "You're not. You know you're not."

She sighed. "Everyone at the law firm knew I wouldn't respond to any damn emails or text messages after 7:00 PM and that Greg and the kids were my number one priority. I always made time for him and the kids. Even when I was tired as hell from work, I would come home, cook dinner, help with homework, put the kids to bed, shower and make love to him like nobody's business. Yet that wasn't enough."

She began coughing uncontrollably, and I handed her a glass of water. After the coughing subsided, she took a moment to collect her thoughts before resuming.

"I found credit card receipts for flowers and lavish gifts. Here I was, thinking he was at the firehouse and he was in her bed. I confronted him about it, and he came clean. He told me everything about the affair and the birth of their son."

The pain in Elena's voice clogged my throat with emotion.

"Greg is not off the hook for what he's done to our family," she continued. "You hear me. I had to seriously pray about it, and I asked God to help me forgive him. I made it perfectly clear to Camille that I was not pleased knowing she had been sleeping with my husband. But at the end of the day, it's not her fault. I'm married to Greg, not her."

Elena suddenly stopped mid-sentence and began to cry inconsolably. "I realized I had to put my feelings to the side and think about my babies first. I won't be here to protect them, but she will."

Chapter 9

Which Way is Up

I found great joy in watching Malik sleep. I was struck by his flawless caramel skin. His broad shoulders sprawled across the bed, revealing intricate tattoos on his chest and defined six-pack that resembled the language of hieroglyphics, weaving their own tale. His tattoos were usually hidden beneath clothing so I felt privileged to witness them up close.

I sat up with the sheets wrapped around my bare body, and I thought about my future with Malik. I'd never been so happy with a man in my life until I met him. It was so easy to love him, and I couldn't imagine life without him.

Before I met Malik, life seemed so ordinary and uninspiring. But since then, every moment with him was like waking up to a dream. When we were apart, all I could think about was when I was going to see him next.

I recalled our first date at the restaurant as if it was yesterday. The way he looked at me with his captivating brown eyes and the sound of his laughter made me feel like I was the only person in the room. I knew from that moment that I wanted to spend the rest of my life with him.

As I watched him breathing peacefully, I couldn't help but wonder what our future would hold. Would we get married, have kids, travel the world? The possibilities were endless, but one thing for sure was that as long as I had Malik by my side, life would be just fine.

I leaned over and planted a soft kiss on his full lips, and he opened his mouth just enough to slide his tongue into mine. He pulled me closer to him, and I snuggled down into the covers with his arms wrapped around me, feeling blessed for this moment of pure bliss.

***

Thanksgiving was a few weeks away, and I felt a surge of excitement from everywhere. Stores were already filled with Christmas trees decorated with flashy, colorful ornaments and twinkling Christmas lights. The scent of pine and vibrant poinsettias added to the ambiance. Malik and I had decided to rent an Airbnb until after the New Year, which meant that he would go back to Costa Rica after Thanksgiving and return before the holidays.

I was thrilled that he was traveling with Maverick during Christmas. My heart melted when Malik told me how badly Maverick was missing me and that he only slept on my side of the bed. I couldn't wait to see my pooch again.

Elena and I put together the menu for an early Thanksgiving feast. Greg and Elena both came from big families, plus an extended family of close friends. Elena wanted to make sure they had time with both sides, so we planned the meal in a way that brought everyone together. I took care of the meat and poultry dishes while she handled the vegetarian options, sides, and pies. When she became tired, I took over. Almost everything was cooked except for the collard greens.

Camille arrived bright and early with Greg's son Gavin in tow, who was a miniature and lighter-skinned version of Greg. "It smells so good in here," Camille exclaimed as she hugged Elena. Elena stopped what she was doing and gave Gavin a huge kiss.

While the children were playing, Camille attentively watched Elena as she meticulously cleaned and trimmed the greens. A perplexed expression appeared on Camille's face as she observed Elena's assembly line breakdown of washing the collards with vinegar and rinsing them multiple times.

I chimed in. "Camille, it's essential to wash the greens meticulously as they may have bugs or dirt on them." Though she appeared to be shocked at how much work it took to prepare one pot of collard greens, Camille nodded in agreement.

All the food had been cooked and set on warmers by noon, and they were placed throughout the expansive kitchen island connected to the living room. To add to the festive ambiance, charcuterie boards filled with an assortment of fruit and cheeses were set out for everyone to enjoy.

Elena took a brief nap and was up and dressed before the guests arrived. She looked absolutely stunning wearing an off-the-shoulder cream dress with brass earrings and bracelets. She wore a wig that closely resembled her natural hair, leading most guests to believe that her hair had grown back. I noticed how even Greg couldn't keep his eyes off her.

Hannah and Mike arrived, wearing matching ugly Christmas sweaters. As Hannah leaned in for a hug, the scent of alcohol on her breath hit me like a ton of bricks.

Shortly thereafter, Roxanne and her boyfriend Scott arrived. Hannah greeted everyone except for Camille, and I prayed silently that this small interaction was not a sign of drama to come.

Maya and Kevin, who also joined us, sat across from each other, and Pastor Timothy sat at the head of the table with Greg's dad at the opposite end.

We lowered our heads in a moment of prayer. The pastor took the lead while Malik held my hands tightly. The children's voices could be heard in the next room as dinner was being served to them.

As everyone began to eat, the room filled with a symphony of conversation and laughter. Dinner was a feast for the senses. The aroma of Elena's cooking filled the air, and the plates were filled with delectable dishes that we spent hours preparing, including roasted chicken, creamy mashed potatoes, crisp green salads, and a variety of colorful vegetables. Everyone boasted how delicious the collard greens tasted. Glasses clinked as everyone cheered to good conversation and great company.

During dinner, various conversations flowed. Maya and Kevin, who had just returned from their honeymoon, shared stories of their travels abroad. Roxanne and I reminisced about our college days, sharing inside jokes and laughter. Greg's dad had everyone cracking up with tales from his younger years, keeping everyone entertained with his wit and charm.

Camille, however, seemed withdrawn throughout the evening. Her blue eyes roamed the table, avoiding direct eye contact with anyone. It was obvious that something was bothering her, and I hoped it wouldn't disrupt the vibe of our gathering.

Malik noticed her uneasiness as well and made a conscious effort to engage her in conversation, trying to alleviate any tension she might be feeling. Slowly, a smile crept across Camille's face, and she began to open up and appeared more at ease.

Have you given Camille a tutorial on how to braid Kniya's hair yet?" Hannah, slightly tipsy from one too many glasses of wine, asked.

Mike gently placed his hand over Hannah's, silently urging her to stop. She aggressively pulled her hand away, and the room fell into an uneasy silence as Hannah struggled to compose herself.

"I actually know a thing or two about braiding Black hair," Camille announced.

Hannah, with a tinge of sarcasm, replied, "Let me guess. This is not your first time at the rodeo? You've broken up a few happy homes?"

Roxanne nearly choked as she excused herself, needing to use the bathroom.

"That's enough, Hannah," Greg shouted in frustration.

Hannah stood, brandishing her fork in Greg's face, revealing her freshly French manicured nails. The scene was reminiscent of the famous moment between Celie and Mister in the classic film *The Color Purple*.

"Greg, never mind me. You just keep that stray over there on a leash," she yelled.

Greg remained silent but was visibly upset as the bulging vein on his forehead became noticeably prominent, and Elena began crying and pounded her hands on the table before storming out of the room.

Malik discreetly glanced over at Mike, who then politely expressed his gratitude for the delicious meal. "Dinner was fantastic, but we'll be heading out early."

I don't want to go yet," Hannah pouted, slumping back into her seat, shaking the table and taking a corner of the tablecloth with her. Her abrupt action almost tipped a bowl of cranberry sauce, her glass of wine and her dinner plate over. Everyone held on to the tablecloth to avoid a spill and stared at Hannah as though they were watching a slow-moving train wreck unfold.

"Can you pass me some cornbread?" Hannah asked. Someone did, and after taking a bite, Hannah shouted, "This is delicious, Tiff! Jiffy? Girl, you put your foot in this. Babe, you want some?" she asked, turning to Mike.

"I had some already, thanks," he said sheepishly as he lowered his head in embarrassment.

An air of silence sat heavily over the room with a mix of confusion and curiosity. Hannah reached for another piece of cornbread and slathered mounds of butter until a small voice broke through.

Gavin, the son of Camille and Greg, approached Camille and affectionately extended his hands, yearning for her to lift him into her lap. He then made his way over to Greg, asking, "Daddy, soda?"

Greg's dad dropped his fork on his plate and rose abruptly. "Son, can you fill me in as to what the hell is going on?"

Before he could respond, Camille abruptly left the room while Gavin followed behind her.

Greg sighed. "Dad, please, let's talk later."

Maya and Kevin exchanged puzzled glances, uncertain of what they actually heard and what had transpired.

Kevin said, "Maya and I still have a few more stops before we head home, so…" Maya nodded awkwardly in agreement.

A silent beat followed, and then the pastor said, "I need to get going as well." He took his last gulp of wine and placed his napkin over his plate.

As the mood shifted, people slowly stood up from the table and began collecting their belongings. Elena expressed her apologies to her guests, and one by one, they exchanged warm farewells, embracing each other and making plans to meet up soon. At the doorstep, Elena stood somberly, waving goodbye to everyone.

While Roxanne and I helped Elena clean up after dinner, we couldn't stop talking about Hannah's drunken behavior at dinner and Greg's dad's reaction after learning about his grandson.

Elena shook her head. "I thought he'd told his family. Camille didn't seem too happy about it." Elena shifted the conversation back to Hannah. "Did you see how much she was drinking?"

"She's drinking entirely too much," I said.

"I tried to get her attention, but she wouldn't look my way," Roxanne added.

***

A few weeks passed, and Hannah had not returned any of our calls for weeks. Even Mike, who was away on business, had not heard from her. We made sure to check on her the only other way we knew how and that was by watching her anchor the news. Seeing her there, we knew she was at least alive and apparently well enough to perform her job. Elena suggested that we give her some space and that, eventually, she would come around. We all agreed to respect Hannah's space.

Then, one Sunday afternoon, she showed up at Elena's house during our usual brunch time. "Hey, bitches! Did you miss me?" she shouted.

We looked at each other, and for a moment, we were stunned. Then excitement came over us, and we all burst out in laughter.

Chapter 10

Uptown Saturday Night

It had been quite some time since I last had the pleasure of going out dancing in an American club, and the anticipation had me overwhelmed with excitement. Dancing had always been my chosen escape, a means to let loose, flirt, get my drink on, and get some cardio in. I was eager to shed some of the few unwanted winter pounds I had gained while being in Atlanta. However, my man had no issues with me being a little thick in all the right places. He liked being able to hold on to something at night.

This night was extra special. Roxanne was celebrating her promotion as Director of Diversity and Inclusion at Price Cooper Waterhouse. This was a huge deal, and I couldn't have been happier for her.

Roxanne's sleek Benz cast a radiant glow, piercing through the expansive floor-to-ceiling bay windows that adorned the entire rental home located in a quaint neighborhood in Buckhead. The rhythmic bass of Beyoncé and Meg Stallion's remix "Savage" reverberated throughout the entire house as Roxanne pulled into the driveway.

She beeped the horn, with her headlights beaming on me. I came out strutting like I was on someone's runway and wearing fitted black leather pants and a light black wool top that fell slightly off my shoulder with my signature hoops dangling from my ears.

My love for wearing hoops dated back to the days of watching Janet Jackson's videos, and I have been hooked ever since.

The Atlanta night air held a refreshing chill, far more temperate compared to the bone-chilling winters I had endured in New York City. The mere thought of venturing out during this time of year in New York City was unbearable.

When I entered the car, Roxanne and I embraced each other. "Hey, diva! So how does it feel to add more zeros to that paycheck?"

"Girl, I love it." Roxanne smiled from ear to ear. "I truly believe this is where I'm supposed to be. I was nervous about taking this huge leap, but I prayed about it, and Scott has been so supportive. They say depending on where the country is leaning politically, those are the first positions to be eliminated. My company is deeply committed to creating a team atmosphere that is felt across the board. You know what they say, don't just invite me to the party—ask me to dance." We burst out in laughter and high-fived each other.

"I am so proud of you."

"Thanks, girl."

"How are things with you and Scott?"

"Great. I couldn't have asked for a better man. I really believe he could be the one." When I raised a brow, Roxanne said, "No, seriously. He's so encouraging. I mean, I can talk to him about anything."

Roxanne switched her attention to me and asked, "How about you and Malik?"

"Perfect. Really. I mean, we have no issues."

"Well, I'm sure at times the distance apart can be tough."

"Of course, but we love each other so much that I don't believe the Titanic, broken down in the middle of the Atlantic, could separate us.

"First off, Bish, yo ass can't swim anyway," Roxanne said in her NOLA accent. We laughed so much that tears kept flowing down our faces long after we stopped talking.

We pulled into a strip mall parking lot where the club stood nestled between a liquor store and a rib shack. A line of eager club-goers awaited their turn to place their orders. The parking lot was filled with cars displaying license plates and bumper stickers from Spelman, Morehouse, Clark Atlanta, Morris Brown, and even a few from Georgia State. It was clear that the club was a hotspot for alumni from the Atlanta University Center.

"Do you see Hannah's Range Rover?"

"No, but the news just ended, and the station is about thirty minutes away. Let's go inside and get us a table."

As we entered the packed and dark, posh nightclub, we saw a perfect spot, a table on the side not too far from the entrance, where Hannah could easily find us. The DJ was spinning classic R&B with a twist of nineties hip-hop. It was a mature crowd, mostly men and women ages thirty-five and over. They were definitely Atlanta's bougie crowd: the transplants from New York to the Bay Area who wreaked havoc on the I-285 morning commute and caused the housing market in Atlanta to quadruple in the last decade or more.

Before I could get settled into my seat, a man who appeared to be in his early fifties, strikingly resembling someone's handsome, younger-looking uncle, extended his hand for me to dance with him. He smelled so good that I couldn't refuse.

We danced to a few songs, during which he expressed to me that I moved my hips like they do in the movies and even offered to take me home with him. Even though I told him about the man I left at home, he insisted that I call him sometime and handed me his business card. By the time I returned to our table, Roxanne was on the dance floor with an attractive, tall man with a rich chocolate complexion and a salt-and-pepper beard.

It was after midnight, and Hannah had not arrived yet. While I was attempting to send her a message, I suddenly felt a tap on my shoulder. It was a waitress offering me a drink from a guest. I politely declined and continued texting. The waitress insisted that the gentleman wouldn't take no for an answer, and she gestured toward him. To my surprise, it was my ex, Langston.

At that moment, my heart skipped a beat or two or three, and heat rose to my cheeks. He approached me, and we hugged for what felt like an eternity. As much as I hated admitting it, I didn't want to let him go.

We spent the rest of the night dancing together. Every now and then, he would jokingly spin me around, causing me to surrender into his arms. We both looked silly, but for some reason, I didn't care how we looked to others. We were in each other's presence, and that was all that mattered to me.

As he lifted me from a dip, our lips met, and I couldn't bring myself to resist his kiss, although a wave of guilt overwhelmed me as I grappled with the disbelief of what I had just done. How would I tell Malik? I wanted to hide under a boulder.

As I approached Roxanne, the worried look on her face caught my attention. "What's the matter?"

"I just spoke with Elena." For a moment there, I thought the emergency was about Elena. "Hannah has been arrested for a DUI."

"Are you kidding me?"

"No, and we need to hurry to the police station."

"Where is she?"

"Gwinnett County Police station." I turned to Langston, gave him a hug and told him that I would catch up with him later. Roxanne and I belted out of there.

While we made our way to the police station, Elena called and spoke to us on speaker to inform us of what we could expect.

"John Gibson, my mentee from the office, will be meeting you guys at the station," she explained.

I asked if there was anything she needed from us.

"No, John is an excellent attorney and will take care of everything, including getting her released on bond. Her Range Rover has been impounded. I've also been told that she hasn't been processed yet, so we'll have to wait for that before she can be bonded out. I've also contacted our Crisis Management PR firm, which is keeping an eye on the situation and preparing a draft response for Hannah. Just hang in there, ladies. It's going to be some time before she's released."

"When will she see the judge," I asked.

"Most likely not until Monday. Well, ladies, I am heading back to bed now. Give me a call if you need me. Love you all," Elena reassured us.

"Get some sleep. Love you, Elena," Roxanne said, then turned to me. "Should we call Mike?"

"I don't know. They've been on the outs for a few weeks now. Let's wait to see what Hannah says."

I was astounded by Elena's strength. Despite being incredibly ill, she remained on top of everything. This should have come as no surprise, of course. After all, she was a Virgo and graduated at the top of her class from Howard Law School.

Roxanne and I rode to the police station practically in silence. The only voice that could be heard in the car was Joyce Littel from V103 on the *Quiet Storm*.

That is, until I blurted out, "Tonight at the club, I kissed Langston."

"Really?"

"Yes."

"Please don't tell me you plan on telling Malik."

"You think I shouldn't?"

"Just for a kiss? Tiff, your relationship is going well. Keep it to yourself. Do you want to be with Malik?"

"Yes. I love him. Of course, I do."

She glanced over and, I assume, noticed my puzzled expression because she next asked, "So what's the hesitation?"

"Seeing Langston brought back so many fond memories, I couldn't help but smile."

Roxanne chuckled. "You're horny. When is Malik coming back?"

"Toward the end of next week."

"You'll be okay. But you should reevaluate your relationship and figure out what's really going on with you."

"Why do you say that?"

"Earlier, you said everything was perfect, yet after a few drinks, you couldn't resist kissing your ex."

"Yes. You're right."

We fell into silence again, but it didn't last long. "Oh no! I just received a notification on my phone."

"What's wrong?"

"Langston just sent me a request to connect on LinkedIn. What should I do?"

"Go ahead and connect, but make it clear that you're madly in love with your man."

I was in deep thought with everything that was happening. As someone who has gone through significant life changes, Atlanta remains a city of mixed feelings for me. It was where I pursued my higher education and eventually lived before settling back into Snowville and ultimately establishing residency in New York City. However, my heart ached for Langston, my first love, who I deliberately left behind in Atlanta.

I had never imagined, in a million years, that I would run into him in a nightclub, of all places. He wasn't the club type, at least not back then.

I thought that chapter of my life was closed, and for valid reasons. However, the love I once had for him remained deeply ingrained in my heart. Roxanne was right in urging me to uncover the truth about my current situation.

When we arrived at the police station, we observed a bustling lobby filled mainly with Black and brown women of all ages, including grandmothers who attentively tended to their grandchildren. John introduced himself and told us about the prolonged waiting period before her release, so we left and returned bearing lattes from Starbucks.

Roxanne and I waited patiently in the lobby for another hour. It was 3:00 AM when we went back to the car to rest. Around 6:30 AM, John tapped on the window and told us she was coming out.

We stood patiently in the chilly weather, standing by the building's side, awaiting her release. Finally, she emerged and embraced us tightly, as if her life depended on it. A lone photographer came out of nowhere and began snapping photos of Hannah. John motioned the photographer to move out of the way and quickly escorted her to the car.

Tears had reddened her eyes, causing her eyeliner and mascara to stream down her face. After thanking John, she swiftly joined us in the car as we headed off to Elena's.

We all waited patiently for Hannah to finish showering, get dressed, and join us for breakfast. What she didn't know was that our meeting was a planned intervention. Elena had a good way of finding out things. Turns out that this was Hannah's second DUI. The first time, the officers on the scene recognized her from the news and issued her a warning. She wasn't allowed to drive home, and her car had been towed.

I predicted this conversation could go in either direction. It could blow up in our faces with her storming out and never speaking to us again. I had a million-and-one questions to ask her. Elena even pulled out a notepad to offer counsel on enrolling her in a diversion program or a drug and alcohol program for offenders. I just wished she would hurry up before the Crisis PR team arrived. I also had a call due out to Malik. He was concerned about Hannah as well and called as we were pulling into Elena's driveway. I told him I loved him and that I would call him back as soon as I had a chance.

Hannah took a seat, wearing no makeup and her hair neatly pulled back in a ponytail, sporting a gray Howard Law School sweatshirt paired with faded blue denim jeans. A hint of strawberry-scented hair gel permeated around her. She had a worried look on her face. I suppose she knew we had questions based on the concerned look on our faces.

Elena held her hand, and Hannah began crying. "If you're wondering, I don't have a drinking problem."

"You effectively have two DUIs," Elena said. The fact that we were aware of the first one appeared to have caught Hannah off guard.

"My life feels like it's spinning out of fucking control. The new director, Jim, has called me into his office repeatedly over the past few months, hinting that higher-ups are considering removing me from the evening news to Daybreak."

"What does that mean?"

"I would have to report the news during the early morning newscast."

"While everybody is sleeping? Oh, hell no," I said.

"He constantly criticizes my performance as a journalist. He scrutinizes everything from my attire to my hair."

"What about your hair?" I asked.

"I wanted to try something different, so I wore my hair curly."

"I remember that," Elena said. "It looked beautiful." Roxanne nodded in agreement.

"Viewers wrote in and expressed how much they loved my hair. Even Tim, my co-anchor, commented on air about it."

"Hell, it made the national news," Roxanne threw in as she rolled her eyes in disbelief.

"Well, Jim mentioned that the emails he received were not favorable and that it was important to maintain a corporate image. He pointed out that my current hairstyle might affect the viewership, and as a team player, he advised me to reconsider wearing my hair straight."

Elena reminded Hannah about the Crown Act, and Hannah said, "Yes, but I need my job, so I go to Carla, my Dominican hair stylist, to have my hair blow-dried straight."

"How does Mike feel about all of this?"

"Mike and I are no longer together," Hannah said as her eyes began to fill up quickly with tears. She then went back to discussing her problems at the job.

"Jim told me that I'm partial in my reporting toward people of color, particularly Black women when it comes to asking the tough questions. And why? Because I was assigned to cover a breaking news story. The woman we interviewed was still sleeping when we got there, so I politely asked if she needed a moment to gather herself. I didn't want her looking crazy on air. Besides, she had just lost her son from a shootout with the police.

"Everything went smoothly, and we managed to capture the live shot on time. The real problem is that she refused to speak to anyone from the station except for me. And to top it off, the production assistant told me that he caught Jim a few times rummaging through my desk when I'm not around."

Hannah sighed and went on. "With all these issues, I'm afraid I might not have a job come Monday morning."

"It sounds like you're having a Phillis Wheatley moment," Elena suggested.

"What do you mean?"

"Are you referring to the American poet?" Roxanne asked.

"She was enslaved, right?" I chimed in.

Yes, Phillis Wheatley became one of the first Black women to document her story in an autobiographical book called *Life of a Slave Girl* in *1773*. No one believed or could have imagined that a Black woman could have the level of intelligence to write a book. She had to stand up to a crowd of naysayers to prove her worth. Her talent was questioned and doubted by biased white men.

"This is what we've coined a Phillis Wheatley moment."

"Sounds about right," Hannah said with a nod as she looked around the table at all of us.

I quickly raised my hand like a kid in a classroom. "I think it's safe to say we've all been down that road at some point or another. Every roadblock I've experienced in my career as a software engineer has been met with unfair skepticism.

***

The crisis PR team managed to gain possession of the photos taken of Hannah by a photographer during her release from jail. Frank Ski on the V103 radio station asked listeners to pray for Hannah. They mentioned that she was going to make an announcement on air that evening. Listeners were calling in, expressing how much they admired Hannah's community involvement and that they hoped she was not leaving the station for good.

Roxanne, Elena and I were on a call together and glued to our TVs as we watched Hannah deliver an apology on air about her recent DUI arrest.

"In journalism school, we're taught not to be the subject of our story. Unfortunately, I am the story today. This is why I feel compelled to address you, the viewers, directly.

I owe you an apology along with my colleagues, Mera Corporation, friends and family. Recently, I made a serious lapse in judgment and have been charged with driving under the influence. I am deeply sorry for my actions, as they do not reflect the values I hold or the responsibility I have as your news anchor. It is my sincere commitment to rectify this situation and take the necessary steps to make amends.

I will be taking a short leave of absence to ensure I attend to my personal matters responsibly. I genuinely appreciate your support and understanding during this time, and I promise to return as soon as possible, fully committed to delivering the news with the professionalism and dedication you expect. Thank you for your understanding."

We were so proud of Hannah. It was one of the hardest things she had ever had to do in her career.

The initial feeling of embarrassment gradually diminished as an outpouring of support from viewers and colleagues across the nation started flooding in. Bouquets and kind wishes were sent her way.

Hannah had earned the respect of her peers long before she became a news anchor. She had been a devoted member of NABJ, the National Association of Black Journalists, since college. In addition, she earned six News Emmys throughout her career to prove it.

Hannah entered a posh rehabilitation program in Arizona, one of the best in the country. She was scheduled to be released sometime after the holidays. During the first few weeks, she couldn't have visitors, calls, or access to email. However, we eventually reached her to see how she was doing and learned that she was well and that Mike had been in touch.

She also heard from Jim, who was incredibly kind to her over the phone, and he shared with her that everyone at the station was rooting for her and eagerly anticipating her return. Interestingly enough, her co-anchor told her that the ratings had dipped since she had been away.

Chapter 11

She's Gotta Have It

Langston entered the swanky bistro with so much swag that everyone turned to look his way. His aura of confidence captivated everyone in the room, including a small group of waiters, who were huddled around the register in a corner behind my table, whispering and trying to identify who he was. Each step he took emanated a sense of undeniable charm and charisma, causing heads to turn and conversations to cease. Not to mention, he wasn't too shabby on the eyes.

Hailing from the Southside of Chicago, Langston had not changed much from college. His boyish-looking charm never faded away with age. Langston was of medium height with a tawny complexion, dimples and broad shoulders, similar to an MLB player. A speckle of gray on his goatee and his hair gave him an added sense of authority.

Langston was greeted by one of his fraternity brothers as he walked into the restaurant. His friend was accompanied by what appeared to be his family. Langston wore a designer tan sports jacket, a powder blue button-down shirt, denim jeans, and brown Florsheim shoes. As soon as he noticed me, he said goodbye to his friend and quickly walked over to the table. He gave me a huge hug.

He had on my favorite cologne, Sauvage, by Dior. As he sat across from me, a continuous smile graced his face, and he gazed into my eyes.

The heat of a blush struck my cheeks, and I asked, "What?"

"You look fantastic."

"Thank you. You do, too."

"I've missed you so much, Tiffany," he said while holding my hands. "After that night at the club, I couldn't stop thinking about you. What have you been up to lately? Last time we spoke, you mentioned something about heading off to New York City, and then you ghosted me. Your number changed. Did you ever get the job you were after?"

"You have a good memory."

"So, you do recall ghosting me?"

"Not quite."

We laughed, and the waiter came by with a menu and water. After he stepped away, I replied, "Yes, I did get the job."

We talked and laughed for more than an hour. After we left the restaurant, we went roller skating, where we spent hours skating to our favorite tunes from the nineties. What a sight to see as Langston serenaded me, dancing to the song "Can We Talk" by Tevin Campbell. He pretended to hold a microphone in his hand as he did a two-step, attempting to do a fancy turnaround. He stumbled and fell to the floor while skaters zipped past him.

I couldn't control my laughter and nearly fell as I grabbed onto the nearest railing to avoid falling myself. We collided multiple times throughout the night and broke out in laughter, causing the other to tumble. I had bruises to show for it the next day.

Langston was comedic and had an infectious laugh that could make anyone burst out in joy, just as I remembered. It had been a long time since I'd had so much fun.

We ended the night ordering cheeseburgers, fries, onion rings, and strawberry milkshakes from The Varsity, our favorite hangout place while in college. We remained in the car as they delivered our food. Langston puffed on a cigar as he talked mostly about his tech company, I-HBCU, that he and his classmates from Morehouse founded. Langston was a serial entrepreneur to the core and had a few successful and failed businesses, but I respected his hustle. In college, he saved his money and, along with a few friends, began print-screening their own T-shirts with popular slogans they then sold on campus.

He explained that their silent partners were two NBA players whose names I didn't recognize. They had given Langston and his partners their initial seed money to start the business. At this point, the business valuation was estimated to be close to five million.

"So, I'm good for a loan?" I asked jokingly.

"Not yet, but soon."

"Okay, I'm going to hold you to that." I laughed. "I am so proud of you."

"Thank you," he said while grinning from ear to ear and exposing his pristine white veneers.

Langston's demeanor suddenly changed. He turned to me in a serious manner and looked me directly in the eyes. "You know, I could do this with you every day."

I couldn't help but smirk in response. "Really?"

He nodded. "No, seriously. Since I ran into you at the club, I don't know what to do with myself. All I think about is you. I believe you're the one that got away. Tiff, I ain't bullshitting you either."

I couldn't believe what I was hearing. For years, I wondered the same. Was he the love that slipped away?

I felt vulnerable inside, and I couldn't muster a response. I wasn't emotionally prepared for all of this. Not tonight. So, instead, I listened to what he had to say.

"Tiff, I never stopped loving you. I don't know what happened between us."

You never wanted to settle down, I thought to myself.

"I've even prayed for this day to come."

No, he didn't just say he prayed about it. I never knew him to be the spiritual type, and this was really pushing it.

Just as he confessed his love for me, my phone lit up, and a photo of Malik appeared on my screen, signaling an incoming call. I quickly sent it to voicemail, hoping to continue this moment undisturbed. Malik followed up with a text that he was heading to bed and that he loved me, asking me to give him a call in the morning.

I knew I had to come clean with Langston. As much as I adored him, I couldn't give him false hope of us getting back together because I only saw a future with Malik.

On the following day, I went by to see Elena. I was excited to share with her my time with Langston. I was shocked to see how much weight she had lost just from the last time I saw her. Her eyes had sunken in, and her collarbone protruded. She was pale and appeared exhausted.

She was still lying in bed, which was unusual for her at this time of day. The shades were closed in her room, too.

"Did the nurse not come today?" I asked.

"Yes, she did, and I asked her to leave the drapes closed."

"Are you feeling okay?"

"I'm just tired, and I have a migraine."

"Have you taken anything for it?"

"Yes, I believe so. I'm sure it's just because I was up late wrapping presents for the kids."

I settled in to keep her company for a while and told her about my date with Langston.

"Who?" she asked a few times, and I repeated that information. She vaguely remembered him, which was odd because she was with me when I first met him in front of our dorm. She also knew intricate details about our past relationship.

Concerned about her sudden coughing fit, I handed her a glass of water. She asked if I could hand her a notepad from her nightstand. It had a reminder note for her to ask me if I could pick up the kids from school due to early dismissal.

I left her home in tears. Seeing my best friend literally deteriorate in front of my eyes was truly heart-wrenching.

It was in those moments I feared the most that Elena was nearing her death.

I immediately called Malik, who stepped out of his meeting to take my call. I was sobbing and struggling to get a word out.

"Tiffany, what's the matter? Babe, I can't understand you."

"I saw Elena, and she didn't look well at all. She couldn't remember some of the things I was telling her. This is just too much for me to handle."

Malik put me at ease, and he urged me to stay present. He emphasized the importance of me cherishing every precious moment I had with Elena.

After my conversation with Malik, I immediately called Elena and told her I loved her. In typical Elena fashion, she asked me if everything was okay with me, and I told her yes. Then, she reciprocated by expressing her love for me.

***

While I was disappointed that Malik and I weren't spending the holidays together in Atlanta as we had initially planned. My sadness didn't last long, as our New Year's Eve plans were still on track.

His mom was struggling with her diabetes: her blood sugar numbers had spiked, and the doctor ordered her to rest. His sister and her family were celebrating Christmas with Malik's parents.

After dropping off everyone's presents, I heard from Hannah and couldn't resist laughing at her stories about the people she was meeting there. I knew we would never hear the end of it. I was relieved, though, that my bestie sounded like herself again.

Mike and Hannah were on better terms and were planning to spend Christmas together in spite of a 10:00 PM curfew set by the facility.

Roxanne and Scott were spending their first Christmas together, and Langston was heading off to be with family in Chicago. Elena and Greg were spending a quiet Christmas at home with their kids.

As for me, I was spending Christmas alone.

Chapter 12

Jason's Lyric

I woke up to a throbbing headache and a runny nose. The constant need to blow my nose led me to keep a roll of toilet paper within arm's reach and a piece conveniently lodged in one nostril.

I managed to find the strength to get up, and I dragged my aching body toward the winding stairs with a bottle of Tylenol in hand. I stood for a moment, paralyzed in thought and blinded by the shining sun as it forced its way through the floor-to-ceiling windows. I couldn't believe it was Christmas. The only evidence of the holiday was a poinsettia gifted to me by Elena that sat alone on the mantle above the fireplace.

I looked out the window, and a white van pulled into the driveway. I couldn't read the letters on the van before it came to a stop. A minute later, a man appeared on my doorstep, his hands burdened with two massive bundles of vibrant red roses. I was overcome with emotion and hastily opened the door.

"Tiffany Myers?"

"Yes, that's me."

"Merry Christmas." He handed off the two huge, beautiful bouquets of red roses.

Taking a deep breath, I inhaled the intoxicating fragrance from the roses and read the card from Malik. *"I love you, Tiffany. Merry Christmas."*

I was so happy that I immediately dialed his number. As we spoke, Malik told me how much he loved me. He explained that he had a busy day ahead of him and expressed his regret for not being able to be there in person. However, he was looking forward to us bringing in the New Year together.

I gently sipped on my tea while leisurely scrolling through a flood of text messages sent by friends and family laden with cheerful emojis like snowflakes, reindeer and vibrant-looking snowmen with bright red hats, all wishing me a Merry Christmas.

Just as I was preparing to return to bed, Langston called. He missed his flight the night before, he explained, and wanted to hang out.

I told him I was sick and that I would talk to him later. He insisted on coming by to help me out, but I declined, knowing I needed some rest.

Eventually, he sold me on the idea of him making me his grandmother's Creole-style homemade chicken soup to nurse me back to health.

I quickly jumped in the shower and threw on my Christmas onesie. I looked haggard and was tempted to crawl back into bed and call him to say never mind.

I took off my pink hair bonnet and tried to gather my freshly tightened box braids into a ponytail, but the tension on my braids was too much to bear, so I left them down. I tucked a few of them on each side behind my ears.

Langston arrived at my door wearing gray sweats with an embroidery of I-HBCU in pan-African colors emblazoned on his sweatshirt. He also wore a red Christmas hat. He had a huge smile on his face and carried a bag full of groceries.

"Merry Christmas," he cheered as he kissed me on the cheek and gave me a gift bag from Tiffany's.

I squealed in excitement. It was a beautiful charm bracelet. We awkwardly hugged each other, and I quickly let go of him. I piled a stack of blankets and pillows around me for extra comfort while Langston made his way around the kitchen.

"Nice roses," he called out.

"Thanks."

I was dosing off when Langston gently tapped me to let me know the food was ready. The aroma of the soup made me eager to dive right in.

"Here you go," he whispered, setting before me a wholesome bowl of chicken soup with tender chunks of poultry, shrimp, crab meat, vegetables and dumplings alongside a slice of toast. The soup was piping hot, so I took a few moments to cool it down by blowing on it. The combination of flavors, including pumpkin, Creole and allspices, made it satisfying.

I could tell Langston wanted to get something off his chest by the way he paced the room. I continued to eat, occasionally pausing to blow my nose.

This continued for about fifteen minutes before I finally asked, "What's wrong?"

He hesitated for a moment before answering, "Nothing."

I chuckled, momentarily interrupted by a fit of coughing. Langston rushed to the kitchen and handed me a glass of ginger ale.

As he handed me the soda, he asked, "What do you think about us getting back together again?" I was taken aback by his statement. He stood before me with crossed arms, seemingly expecting me to say no, as though he could read my mind.

"Langston, I'm in love with a wonderful man whom I plan to marry someday. You're a tad bit late."

"Are you sure about your feelings for him?"

"Yes, I am."

"What about that kiss we shared?"

"What about it?"

"You weren't acting like a woman in love."

"I'd had too many drinks."

"So, you want to blame it on the alcohol," he said with a smirk on his face.

"What is it with you, Langston? Do you want to sleep with me or something? Is that it?"

"Yes, I do."

Well, it didn't take long for the truth to come out.

"Wait a minute," he added, interrupting my thoughts. "I admit we shared some magnificent times together, but our relationship was never based solely on sex. I would hope we had a deeper connection than that. Besides, this is Atlanta, chocolate heaven. I don't need to concoct a story to get sex from you or any woman. I can get it anywhere."

I looked over at him and couldn't help but roll my eyes.

"You know what I mean."

The truth was, I did have some feelings for him, which was causing quite a bit of confusion in my head and left me at a loss for words on how to express myself. How was it possible to have feelings for him and still love Malik?

Pushing those thoughts aside, I'd started to feel a little better, so I took my bowl to the kitchen. After discarding the leftovers in the garbage, I began washing the dishes in silence while passing them off to Langston to dry and put them away in the cabinet.

"Damn, Tiff, life is too short. I mean, I don't want to have any regrets. I know I wasn't good to you back then. I was going through a lot emotionally. My parents ended their marriage, and I was afraid."

"Langston, be honest. You never took our relationship seriously when we dated in college. It showed by the way you treated me. You never made time for me. You were too busy partying with your frat and chasing women. All I ever wanted was to experience love that I didn't have to fight for. That's why I ghosted you."

"How about you?"

"What about me?" I turned the water faucet off so he could hear me clearly. "If you want to know if I cheated on you, the answer is no."

"Each time I visited CC-4, some muscled dude would walk up to my car and ask if I was here to see those college girls?"

"What did you expect? I had roommates. I loved you, Langston, and you were reckless with my heart."

Tears began to form as I tried to gather my thoughts, but I felt depleted. He tried to hold me, but I shrugged him off and continued wiping down the countertop. The truth of the matter was that Langston always felt threatened about me living off campus. His spies had nothing to report.

CC-4 was my first off-campus apartment, more like a rite of passage. Admittedly, it was wild at times. I smoked my first joint and drank mounds of cheap liquor. It was where I lost my virginity to Langston. There were all sorts of episodes of drama between the girls and me, including some heartbreaks, pregnancy scares, grief and trauma, but we managed to get through the best way we knew how somehow unscathed during that awkward time of our lives.

Our tri-level townhouse looked more like a modern-day row house in Philadelphia. It was a fairly new development in a quaint neighborhood that overlooked Peachtree Industrial Boulevard. In the beginning, it was just Hanna and me, and then later Elena moved in shortly afterward because the apartment was near her internship.

One day, Roxanne showed up at our door with suitcases in tow. And as for Greg, he was practically our fifth roommate. Since Elena was the only one who had a steady boyfriend, she got first dibs on the room with the bathroom. She had everything in her room, including a small compact fridge. With the exception of class and her internship, Elena and Greg never left her room.

Our infamous rent parties were the talk of the campus. We crafted a brilliant strategy to meet our rent obligations and then some. We charged ten dollars for the entrance fee. On average, we had close to two hundred college students packed into our small townhouse.

Hanna was the DJ, and she played music from my iPod and connected it to speakers borrowed from Greg. Roxanne accepted the money at the door. We hired our neighbor, an unemployed ex-con, who had an uncanny resemblance to Debo from the movie *Fridays*, giving him a few bucks to make sure nothing got out of hand.

My friend Sam worked at KFC, and he hooked us up with buckets of fried chicken. We concocted our signature punch with cheap liquor, juice and soda bought from The Dollar Store.

At first, Elena showed no interest in the rent party. However, she promptly had a change of heart when she discovered we were making money. She eagerly joined our efforts, but under one condition: everyone had to sign a non-disclosure agreement (NDA) before entering our party.

"I don't want this to come back to haunt me," she said. We were unfamiliar with the concept of an NDA until she explained it to us. Trusting Elena's judgment, we went along with her idea.

We forged a relationship with our neighbors, who were mostly families. They tolerated our monthly parties, mainly because we offered to tutor their children for free. This helped keep the police and property management at bay.

***

"Can we try this again?" he asked while staring directly at my face.

"Langston, I don't want to be dragged along for your convenience. I want to be married and have a family one day."

"What makes you think I don't want that too?" Langston had a disappointed look on his face, and it left me feeling awful.

"I'm not going to wait around to find out. I'm in a healthy relationship, and I think it's best that we remain friends." Saying that left me feeling as though my heart had been ripped out of my chest. For some reason, I wasn't sure if I had made the right decision.

We ended the night playing chess, just like we did in college. The competition between us was so intense that, at times, I felt like Langston saw it as a way to win back my love.

Chapter 13

Antoine Fisher

Hannah was eager to meet up with us upon her return. She couldn't wait to share her experiences from her time away. We dined at a charming new tavern cradled in the heart of Virginia Highlands before heading over to Elena's home.

In this cozy family-run restaurant were a handful of dining patrons, as well as a couple seated at the bar engrossed in conversation. The waitstaff, wearing white shirts and black slacks, meandered throughout the restaurant with grace and efficiency, ensuring each table was properly attended to and the aroma of freshly prepared southern cuisine made its way through the air, enticing everyone's senses.

The walls were painted with a hunter-green accent and rich tones of mahogany wooden fixtures adorned with a collection of paintings that depicted varying aspects of Black life.

Soft jazz music played in the background, adding to the restaurant's charm and creating a warm and inviting atmosphere that the girls and I needed to unwind and catch up.

As soon as we walked in, we were greeted by a young waitress who recognized Hannah from the news. When the host led us to our table, she handed us menus, then leaned toward Hannah and whispered, "Welcome Back."

Hannah smiled and thanked her. Everyone we ran into that day wished her well, and Hannah said it helped her feel appreciated by the Atlanta community.

Hannah sported a new look. She had a sleek, stylish bob haircut that grazed her chin. She wore a camel-colored ribbed sweater with an asymmetrical neckline and matching colored fitted slacks that accentuated her body, which was noticeably lighter in weight, at least ten pounds. She looked well-rested and had a peaceful, serene aura about her.

"So, how do you feel? I asked.

"I feel great."

"You look gorgeous," Roxanne assured her, and I nodded in agreement.

"Thank you, ladies."

"How was your time away?"

"Well…" She sighed. "I learned so much about myself and how to cope with my feelings of unworthiness."

Feelings of unworthiness? I think my facial expression said it all. I looked over at Roxanne for assurance that I heard Hannah correctly. She appeared as stunned as I did by Hannah's revelation, but the last thing I wanted to do was interrupt Hannah's flow, so instead of saying anything, I took a sip of my Sauvignon Blanc wine and listened.

"The therapist believes that it stems from my sexual assault, which I believe over the years has impacted my relationships."

We all drew a blank, her words piercing and the silence at the table deafening. The distant chatter and the sound of utensils hitting against plates echoed throughout the small dinner room.

I sat there dumbfounded, wracking my brain, desperately trying to spark some kind of inspiration to find the right words. Guilt overcame me. We hadn't talked about that fateful day in years, and we continued on with our lives, unaware of the pain Hannah was silently enduring.

The day Hannah was sexually assaulted remained vivid in my mind, as though it happened moments ago. Even the mere mention of it brought back chilling memories that made my stomach churn.

We were all in class on campus except for Hannah, who was at the apartment. She cleverly planned her schedule by combining her classes and work-study into one day to minimize her commute to campus and avoid having to take Marta every day.

We lived far from campus, and the commute on Marta was close to an hour, including the bus ride leaving the station. For the rest of the week, she was either studying in the library or at the apartment.

Hannah had invited Troy, a South Carolina native who attended Georgia State University, over to CC-4. While most of their previous dates had taken place in public, she never feared being alone with him.

Hannah had bought a bookcase for her room, and Troy offered to stop by and assemble it. They had been working on it for nearly an hour when he suggested they take a break. As they were watching TV, he leaned in to kiss her, and she moved her face away. Suddenly, he became agitated and aggressive in his approach.

She told him that she wasn't ready to take their relationship to the next level, but he refused to accept no for an answer and forcefully pinned her down on her bed. She pleaded for him to stop as he placed one hand over her mouth.

She tried everything she could to escape his strong grip, but he easily overpowered her. Her heart pounded in her chest as she realized that time was running out and that she needed to act quickly.

Gasping for air and desperately scanning her room for a way to escape, she made a split-second decision, and when he lifted his body to unsnap her jeans, she quickly rolled over.

With adrenaline coursing through her body, she managed to grab hold of a heavy ceramic vase sitting on the edge of her nightstand, and without hesitation, she swung it toward his head. He ducked, and the vase hit the wall and shattered into pieces. She sprang to her feet and dashed out the door of her room, where she sprinted downstairs to the sounds of his thundering footsteps closing in behind her.

Panic set in as she quickly unlocked the exterior door and ran out into the middle of our complex, screaming at the top of her lungs for help.

A few neighbors came to her rescue as Troy quickly drove away. He was apprehended about a mile down the road. It was revealed in court that he had a history of accosting women on campuses.

Troy was sentenced to ten years in prison. It was definitely a scary time, and we slowed down on hosting the rent parties.

For a while, Hannah was guarded and kept mostly to herself. When she wasn't playing Sade's *Soldier of Love* album on repeat, she was pacing the floors at night, peering out her bedroom window and checking to see if the doors were locked. Eventually, she came around and began acting like her usual self, the feisty Hannah we'd all grown to love.

Several years later, after serving time in prison, Troy was released. He was a registered sex offender who had become an ordained pastor and community activist and had gained notoriety in Atlanta.

He tried multiple times to reach out to Hannah in the newsroom and at home. With no success, he then quietly went on a smear campaign in an attempt to tarnish her reputation, and a judge issued a restraining order against him. Once he realized he was in jeopardy of violating his parole and spending the rest of his life behind bars, the calls and the stalking stopped. Hannah vowed to one day expose his true nature in a future memoir.

***

"Did you talk about Elena's terminal illness with your therapist? Roxanne asked.

"Yes, I did, and she suggested that I take one day at a time."

Elena's health took a dramatic downturn after Thanksgiving. We wanted to spare Hannah from the shock of seeing Elena in such a bad state, as she was now bedridden and reliant on a ventilator.

Hannah paused for a moment to reflect on her progress. "It's so liberating to finally confront my darkest hour that has been cloaked in silence for so long. I'm ready to get back to work and do what I do best: report the news. I don't want you guys to be worried about me. I want you all to know that Elena's illness served as a wake-up call for me, a reminder that life is too short and we mustn't take our physical and mental well-being for granted."

She also boasted about her love for Mike and that their relationship was stronger than ever. Their time apart and also spending Christmas together renewed their commitment to each other.

There was a sense of hope that masked the air as we enjoyed our brunch. Hannah's words showed strength and resilience. Roxanne and I made sure she knew that we would be there to support her on her journey toward healing, offering a shoulder to lean on whenever she needed.

I was so happy for Hannah. She was one step closer to reclaiming the life she desired and deserved.

"How's work coming along," Hannah asked Roxanne.

"It's going well, I guess," she said hesitantly. "I'm not sure if my company is fully prepared to put in the work needed to ensure that everyone at the workplace is seen and heard. At times, I feel as though I'm pushing paper and not doing enough to affect change. Some of the concerns that were brought to my attention and many of my recommendations have not been taken seriously by upper management. But my hands are tied," Roxanne finished, lifting her hands in a gesture of defeat.

"Give it some time," Hannah told her.

"I will. Scott suggested that I hang in there as well."

"So, how are things with the two of you?"

"Fine." Roxanne was smiling so much that I saw all thirty-two of her teeth at once.

I knew something was up with her by the expression on her face, so I asked, "How so?"

"Do you really want to know?"

Hannah took a gulp of her soda and glanced at me for answers. I shrugged in return. I had no clue what Roxanne was up to.

"Scott asked me to marry him."

We screeched so loud that the outburst startled the people at the table next to us, causing them to jump in their seats.

Roxanne proudly placed her left hand on the table for everyone to see her beautiful emerald-shaped diamond ring. We were amazed by its size. We laughed and shed tears of joy for what felt like hours until we were momentarily interrupted by the waitress, who replenished our mimosas; Hannah's was a virgin, of course.

Everyone seated around us congratulated Roxanne on her engagement. I was stunned that they planned to get married so soon, in the spring.

"Are you going to go through the nuptials this time?" I asked.

"Scott is a secure man, and he validates my emotions. He accepts me as I am."

Hannah and I glanced at Roxanne's stomach, wondering if she had another surprise she was keeping from us.

Roxanne quickly clarified, "Oh no, I'm not expecting. Not yet, but it's something we both want right away."

Adjusting her sweater, Hannah said, "Well, I need to hit the gym some more so I can look good for the wedding."

"Yes, me too," I added as we all burst into laughter.

"Is Malik coming up for New Year's Eve?"

Before I could respond, Hannah looked down at her watch and said, "Ladies, we need to get the check. It's almost 2:00 PM. We need to be heading over to Elena's house."

I was relieved that Hannah became distracted. I didn't want to spoil the mood by revealing my drama with Langston and Malik. I wasn't quite prepared to have a conversation with Gail King, or rather, Hannah. She had a knack for asking all the right questions and extracting the necessary answers. My romantic life was not her investigative assignment, and I certainly didn't want her to inadvertently disclose anything to Mike. Besides, my love life should not be treated like a journalistic task.

Things were going smoothly between Malik and me, and the last thing I wanted was to jeopardize what we had.

I did realize too, that he deserved to know the truth from me about my feelings for Langston.

Chapter 14

Mahogany

The heavy atmosphere was filled with sorrow as we gathered around Elena's bedside to say our final goodbyes. One of Elena's dying wishes was to have her dearest friends and family gather and spend her final hour with her. She believed that having her loved ones by her side would bring her comfort and help her face the pearly gates of Heaven with a smile.

Fighting back our tears, we witnessed Elena's genuine joy light up upon seeing us. Her eyes widened as much as they could to acknowledge our presence.

Roxanne proudly showed off her engagement ring, and although Elena attempted to speak, we gently reassured her that we understood her without her having to say the words.

It had finally sunk in that our friend's time with us was rapidly dwindling. We clung to hope for so long that the reality of death seemed distant, only for it to be creeping around the corner. I prayed for a miracle and pleaded to God to spare her from this unbearable fate.

We took turns spending time with her, praying and talking before another group of loved ones entered the room.

Camille came in and greeted us. She tended to Elena with care, hand and foot, and replenished her water. It was the first time I saw Camille in a different light.

In the course of several months, her relationship with Elena blossomed into a friendship, and Elena became more of a confidant to her. I no longer saw Camille as Jezebel, who broke up Elena's happy home by having an adulterous affair with her husband. Instead, I saw a woman who genuinely loved Elena.

I could see that the weight of Elena's impending death was taking a toll on Camille. Her smile seemed forced, and her usually vibrant eyes held a hint of sadness. She gave Elena her meds and immediately left the room.

I followed behind her and called out her name. She turned around and smiled at me kindly, waiting for me to speak.

"Listen, if there's anything you need, I'm here."

"Thank you. Elena has everything. Greg picked up her meds earlier today."

"No, I mean to say if *you* need someone to talk to, I'm here for you."

Camille's eyes welled up in tears. I held her securely, letting her pour out her emotions, offering a comforting presence in her time of need.

As her tears subsided, she said to me, "You don't have to face this alone either. I'll be here for you, Roxanne and Hannah. I know how much she cares about you all."

We stood there, wrapped up in each other's presence, knowing that we had found solace in one another.

Hannah did her best to remain composed, but Roxanne broke down in tears during our conversation about our college escapades and when she showed Hannah a photo of us dressed as the R&B group EnVogue for Halloween.

I could only imagine how Roxanne was feeling at that moment. Elena's impending death had consumed our thoughts and emotions for so long, and now it was really happening. A flood of memories and a mix of both joy and sorrow overcame us.

Both Scott and Mike stopped by to offer their support to Greg, and Malik called multiple times to check in on me. I needed him more than ever, and Friday couldn't come soon enough, so I asked Langston if he could stop by Elena's home. From the urgency of my voice, he knew it was serious, so he came right over.

As Langston arrived, I stood stoic in the foyer, and he greeted me with a concerned expression. "Let's go for a ride," he suggested. I was relieved. I quickly collected my coat and followed him out the door. It was as if he had read my mind.

We drove around the city limits, and I wasted no time before I began sharing with him how I was feeling about Elena dying.

"I don't think it's fair."

"Listen, Tiff. You know Elena would want you to be strong."

"I don't know if I can," I sobbed. "I just don't have it in me anymore."

"It's going to take some time, and if you need me, I'll be here." My mind was all over the place, and I finally had the courage to tell Langston about my feelings for him.

"I'm confused. I do have feelings for you, but I'm also in love with Malik."

"You can't love us both. You have to trust me that I'm not going to hurt you again."

"Are you seeing someone?"

"Yes, but It's nothing serious."

Here we go again. "What do you mean it isn't serious?"

"We've only been dating for a few months, and we're taking things slowly. How about you and Malik?"

"What about him?"

"Have you told him about us?"

"There's nothing to tell."

"Tiff, I love you. I'm not playing. I'm serious."

I looked away from him and took a deep breath, unsure of how to respond. Langston's words weighed heavily on my heart, but a part of me wanted to believe him, to let myself be vulnerable and open to the possibility of us getting back together. But another part of me was like, hell no.

I was still grappling with the heartbreak I suffered years ago when we dated in college. I vowed then that I would never look back.

Could I really trust him again? Could I let myself love him? My mind raced with these questions as I looked into Langston's eyes.

With a crack in my voice, I whispered, "I need time to think, Langston. I need to sort through my feelings and figure out what I really want."

He nodded understandingly. "Take all the time you need, Tiff," he replied softly. "I'll be here for you, no matter what."

At that moment, I knew that this complicated journey of love would require patience and, most importantly, a willingness to trust again, but Malik remained constant in my mind.

As we pulled up to Elena's home, we saw a few people leaving. Langston reached over and kissed me. The warmth of his kiss brought back feelings so deep that I didn't even know they existed. I didn't know what was happening to me, but I couldn't bear to ignore or fight this feeling any longer.

Everyone was so emotionally overwhelmed with Elena that I didn't believe anyone noticed that my ex was by my side. Besides, he was introduced as a friend and not an ex-lover.

Langston knew Greg from when we were dating and quite a few of Elena's friends and colleagues, who were mostly alumni from the AUC. So, it did not come as a surprise to me that Langston knew almost everyone in the house.

The AUC was a part of Atlanta's social fabric, and it was small in nature. If you graduated from Morris Brown, Clark Atlanta, Spelman or Morehouse in the same year or within a few years, it was highly likely that you had some connection with a fellow alum. You either had a class together, dated or competed on rival sports teams. The former mayor herself graduated from Spelman and her husband from Morehouse. This close-knit community was like a members-only club, with a vast network of intertwined lives and shared experiences.

After several hours, more people left, but Roxanne, Hannah and I stayed behind. There were dozens of roses and an assortment of other flower varieties placed everywhere in the room.

Roxanne and I slept on a pullout couch in Elena's room overnight while Hannah made herself comfortable on the leather recliner chair that sat adjacent to Elena's bed.

At around 4:00 AM, Hannah woke us up to tell us that Elena had taken her last breath. I was in a deep sleep, and I felt like I was experiencing a nightmare. I couldn't believe Elena was gone.

Her body was warm, and she looked like she was sleeping, but she was a lifeless shell of her former self. I stood over her in utter shock. I touched her hand to see if she would move, and nothing. I couldn't believe this shit was happening.

With the first rays of sunlight peeking through the blinds, we knew it was time to begin the painful process of spreading the news.

The children entered the room, their attention fixated on Camille's every word. Greg wept uncontrollably while everyone stood back, quietly observing as the coroner somberly carried Elena's body away on a gurney. A heavy silence blanketed us all as the children inquired about their mother's destination and why they couldn't accompany her.

***

I found myself with only an hour left to prepare for the car service that would be picking me up for Elena's funeral. Each time I tried to get out of bed, I was pulled back in. I was emotionally tapped out, and I simply couldn't bring myself to face the reality of saying goodbye. It felt like a heavy weight pressing down on my chest, making it hard to breathe. So, with a deep breath and silent prayer, I slowly pushed myself out of bed and started the difficult task of getting ready.

Malik had arrived the night before. We said very little to each other. As soon as we came in from the airport, we prepared for bed. He was tired from a long flight, and I could hardly keep my eyes open.

Although we made love, I felt something was off between us. My mind was somewhere deep in thought, and I could barely concentrate.

I had hoped he didn't suspect anything or had found out about Langston and me spending time together. I felt a tremendous amount of shame. I loved Malik, and the last thing I wanted to do was hurt him. I just didn't have the courage to tell him.

He held me all night as I tossed and turned and cried throughout the night. I tried to spare him from witnessing the inner turmoil of emotions that plagued my dreams.

As morning arrived, our conversations remained minimal. He showered first and got dressed and then went downstairs and prepared a cup of tea and toast for me, but I had no appetite.

"Babe, try to eat something," he urged me. So, I took a bite of the toast and a sip of the tea, but I couldn't finish the rest.

As I stood before the mirror, trying to make sense of it all, I experienced a profound sadness and felt a huge loss. Even deciding on what to wear was a struggle.

I tried on several different outfits and settled on wearing a black suit jacket with a solid blue draped collar satin blouse, which was Elena's favorite color and a pencil skirt and high heels.

Malik looked over at me and whispered, "You look beautiful."

My hair was pulled back in a sleek bun. I carefully applied my makeup and placed some concealer to hide the bags that sat willfully under my eyes and the tears that had fallen. I made sure I put on Elena's favorite lipstick color, Chocolate Raspberry.

Elena was an old soul. It was a lipstick color from Fashion Fair that her mother wore faithfully while Elena was growing up. It was a richly pigmented hue of magenta, an iridescent pearl that laid perfectly on the lips of melanated women.

In my mind, I could feel Elena's presence guiding me and I imagined her approving my makeup and attire, as she always had a keen eye for fashion.

As the car pulled up outside my door, I took one last look at myself in the mirror. While the pain was still raw, I knew that honoring Elena meant facing my grief head-on. Interestingly, I could almost hear her cheerful voice reminding me that life must go on even in the darkest of times.

Chapter 15

Claudine

A slight overcast hung in the sky, but just as we arrived, the sun broke free from the clouds. It was as though Elena was sending us a sign that she knew we had arrived.

Roxanne, Hannah, and I walked toward the entrance of the church holding hands, bracing for the emotional wave that was about to crash over us. We joined a formal procession led by the pastor, Greg and the children, followed by family members.

A soloist, accompanied by an organist, filled the sanctuary with a beautiful rendition of "His Eye on the Sparrow."

The pews were packed with Elena and Greg's friends and family, classmates from undergrad and law school, neighbors, co-workers, and associates from her law firm, all embracing one another and wiping away tears.

As we walked to our seats, each step was heavy with a mix of grief and nostalgia. A reminder that it wasn't that long ago that we'd marched down this same aisle with most of the people here as a part of Greg and Elena's bridal party.

Elena's lifeless body lay in the casket. She was dressed in a royal blue dress with a brooch that held a photo of her children.

Her face appeared slightly plumper than before, with a peaceful expression that belied the pain and struggles she had endured from her battle with cancer.

Pale pink peony flowers were abundant, just as she had desired, with blooms adorning her casket. I quickly glanced over my shoulder and saw Malik sitting a few pews behind us, along with Mike and Scott, who were pallbearers. Then Camille walked in and I gestured to her to sit next to me, where we sat directly behind the immediate family.

Elena's daughter, Kniya, caught wind that Camille was sitting a few pews behind them and excitedly called out to her, inviting her to join them.

"Camille, come sit with us," Kniya said loudly. "Daddy, Daddy, can Camille sit with us?"

An elderly family member looked back to see what the commotion was and gave Camille a stern look. Greg whispered something to Kniya, and she glanced back at Camille with a sad expression.

Camille silently mouthed, "I'll see you later." Kniya smiled and then rested her head on Greg's shoulder for the rest of the church service.

While Elena had forgiven Greg and accepted Camille, there were some family members of both Elena and Greg who strongly disapproved of Camille. Having Camille sit next to the family during the funeral would've caused mayhem in this small southern Baptist church.

Elena and Greg tried their best to keep Greg's infidelity and love child under wraps, but eventually, the news of their affair got out to most family members.

Elena's family was understandably upset with Greg because they thought of him as the perfect son-in-law, and cheating on Elena was a betrayal of their trust. They couldn't fathom how Greg could cheat on Elena, who was stunningly beautiful and the pinnacle of success, especially for a white woman who, to their knowledge, had no education.

Needless to say, the tension within the family grew out of control as the news continued to spread like wildfire. There were some heated arguments, tearful conversations, and strained family gatherings.

Though Elena attempted to explain her feelings and the genuine bond she grew to have for Camille, it seemed like her pleas fell on deaf ears. Elena hoped that, over time, their families could grow to forgive Greg and accept Camille as her children's future stepmom.

A two-minute documentary-style video played in the background with Elena narrating along with music, chronicling her journey from her childhood to her college years, then law school and on to become a devoted wife and mother.

Family and friends exchanged heartfelt glances, reminiscing about the countless moments they shared with Elena throughout the years. Overwhelmed with emotion, some wiped away tears of pride while others whispered words of admiration for the incredible woman she had become.

Everyone in the church stood while the pastor opened up in prayer. After the eulogy was delivered, a soloist performed a stirring rendition of "Don't Cry for Me" by Bebe and CeCe Winans.

Hannah was called to the pulpit to give her final thoughts. She wore an all-black fitted dress with her hair slicked back and a long layered white pearl necklace.

"Elena and I met in Morris Brown's P.E. class, of all places," Hannah began. "I say this because it quickly became apparent that neither of us was athletically inclined. We spent most days sitting on the gym bleachers, gossiping. Little did we know that this would be the start of an eighteen-year friendship, navigating the ups and downs of life and supporting each other's dreams. We were truly inseparable."

Hannah stopped, almost mid-sentence, and her voice began to tremble with emotion as she tearfully shared stories about Elena's kindness and infectious laughter, painting a vivid picture of the beautiful person Elena was to everyone she met.

"Today, as we lay her to rest, I am grateful to have known her and to call her my sister. Her passing has left a void that will be impossible to fill. But as I look out and see all of you, I know that I am not alone in my grief and that Elena was loved by many. She was one of a kind and made everyone around her a better person. I am going to miss my dear friend and sister.

"Greg, Elena loved you, and I will always be here for you and the kids. To Kniya and Greg Junior, your mom loved you with all her heart. Know that Auntie Hannah will always be here to support you.

"Roxanne and Tiffany, you guys were her extended family, and she loved you both immensely. As we mourn her loss, let's find comfort in the precious memories we shared with her.

"I love you, Elena. Until we meet again."

After Hannah finished her tribute, Greg rose from his seat and made his way to the steps, extending his hand to assist Hannah as she descended the narrow steps from the pulpit, and they embraced.

The pastor ended the service with a final prayer and then led the procession with the casket at the forefront.

The song "I Hope You Dance" by Lee Ann Womack played throughout the church. Roxanne, Hannah and I held one another tighter, finding comfort in our shared grief.

In that moment, it felt as though Elena's spirit remained with us, surrounding us in love and reminding us that she would always be a part of our lives.

As we exited the church, I saw Langston standing and observing everyone. He greeted me with a hug, and I told him the plan for later was to head over to Elena's house.

I told him that Malik was in town and that I would catch up with him later. He walked away disappointed.

It was clear to me that whatever Langston and I were involved in needed to come to an absolute end. It just didn't feel right to do that right then, and I needed to focus on my relationship with Malik.

Elena's repass was positive, and everyone laughed and shared stories. We played music, and some people even danced. As the pastor said, Elena didn't want us to sit back and cry, which was hard not to do, but at the same time, we found comfort in knowing that we were here for each other to celebrate her life.

Despite the obvious tension with Camille, some of Elena and Greg's friends and family went out of their way to make her feel comfortable and offered to help out if needed. Now that Elena was gone, they wanted to be sure her kids would be well taken care of. However, the family was split, and there were many who made it abundantly clear that they did not care for Camille. They simply ignored her as though she didn't exist and talked behind her back. But Camille had tough skin.

Elena warned her of the likely fallout. Some family members believed that Elena's affection for Camille was the result of her impaired mental state due to chemotherapy and pain medication, which we knew was not true. It was just easier to justify Elena's behavior toward Camille.

Greg invited everyone over the next day for brunch and to watch Elena's video diary that she made into a documentary, which we'd only seen a preview of in church during the funeral.

After everyone ate, we all made our way to the spacious theater room with black walls and comfortable adjustable mahogany-colored recliner chairs with padded footrests. Greg had a collection of negro league memorabilia displayed throughout the room, including framed jerseys of Satchel Page, Hank Aaron, Jackie Robinson, Willie Mays, and John Henry Lloyd. A bobblehead of Hank Aaron sat on the bar. An antique popcorn maker adorned with red and white stripes on the side stood in the corner near the entrance of the room, its unmistakable charm adding to the nostalgic flair of the space.

As we settled into the plush, reclining seats, excitement filled the air in anticipation of watching Elena's final words. The room was cozy, with dimmed lights and a large screen that extended from wall to wall. The chatter from friends and family gradually subsided as Elena appeared on screen looking healthy and not as feeble as she did toward the end. It seemed so long ago that we saw Elena this way as we all remembered and loved her.

The sound of crunching popcorn filled the atmosphere, adding to the laughter and gasps that echoed throughout the room. The documentary took us to a different time in Elena's life, captivating our senses with its mesmerizing visuals of the kids as babies, Elena and Greg's wedding and the different stages of their relationship in college and marriage.

Elena opened up about her reality and the significance of her life, expressing her deep love for her children and Greg. A particular aspect that struck a chord with me in the documentary was the realization that if Elena hadn't been facing a terminal illness, she would have fought harder for her marriage. I looked over at Greg, who watched alongside us with tears in his eyes.

Time went by quickly as we laughed, cried, and experienced an array of emotions together. When the documentary ended, everyone expressed their feelings, most bittersweet but grateful for the memories shown and the reality that Elena was no longer among us.

As we said our goodbyes, promising to do it again soon, the aroma of buttery popcorn remained, a gentle reminder of this special moment in time that would forever be etched in our hearts.

***

Malik and I practically rode home in silence. He had been so understanding and supportive, giving me comfort by holding my hand as we made our way through those last few days. His touch was gentle yet firm, reminding me that I was not alone in this. I was grateful for him, and in that moment, I knew he would be there for me through thick and thin.

I was emotionally full and eager to shower, get to bed and sleep. Langston texted me a few times, wanting to see how I was doing, but I didn't respond because I couldn't. I didn't know what to say because my attention was elsewhere.

A part of me wanted to respond, to let him know that I was okay, but another part of me felt overwhelmed and unable to find the right words. It was as if my emotions were in a whirlwind, leaving me tongue-tied and unable to communicate. I knew I had to end things with him.

I walked up the stairs, took off my clothes and entered the shower, where the hot water cascaded down my entire body, relieving the tension that had built up throughout this entire ordeal. In minutes, the bathroom filled with steam and only my silhouette was visible from the shower door.

Stepping out of the shower, I wiped the steamy mirror that stretched along the wall in the bathroom. I wrapped myself in a plush towel, brushed my teeth and made my way to the bedroom. The cool air on my skin was a refreshing contrast to the warmth of the water, and I couldn't help but feel a sense of renewal.

I slipped into an oversized T-shirt, massaged my body with a subtle flowery fragrant blend of lush florals, citrus, and sandalwood, crawled into bed and craved the solace of sleep and the warmth of Malik's body next to mine.

Lying there, my mind continued to race. I realized that I needed to find a way to properly tell Langston that we had to end any thought of us getting back together. It wouldn't be fair for me to leave him hanging, especially after everything we had been through together. I made a mental note to reach out to him in the morning once I had collected my thoughts and found the right words to say.

After taking his own shower, Malik snuggled under the covers with me, his body emanating the calming scent of Dove soap as he held and kissed me all over.

I cried out his name, begging him not to stop. Every time he entered me, I moaned and gasped as our hips swayed in harmony. I turned over, and he slapped my ass a few times as he made his way in. Our bodies intertwined and kept us connected and unbreakable.

This was definitely our love language. We were like acrobats, and with every position he suggested, I was ready to execute it flawlessly.

Our sexual chemistry was unlike anything I had ever experienced. It was as if we were both tuned into the same frequency and voltage. With every move and twist, we seamlessly flowed from one position to another, never missing a beat. The attraction between us allowed for a sense of freedom and excitement, knowing that we could push the boundaries of pleasure while still maintaining a sense of comfort. Together, we created a mesmerizing performance that left us both breathless, proving that when it came to lovemaking, we were bonafide lovers in every sense of the word.

When it was over, I laid my head on his bare, sweaty chest. As a baby hearing its mother's heartbeat for the first time, I drifted off into a peaceful sleep, drawn out of the worry and excruciating pain of loss that had become an intimate part of my life.

At that moment, I felt vulnerable but protected, and I was ready to face whatever the future held.

Chapter 16

Jason's Lyric

Despite repeatedly telling Langston that there was no chance of rekindling a relationship, he insisted that we meet up. Reluctantly, I agreed but felt guilty about deceiving Malik, as I truly wanted to be with him. I told Malik I had a few errands to run and that I would be back home shortly.

Langston had a manipulative hold on me. I was drawn to some sort of magnetic pull toward him that was both infuriating and irresistible at the same time.

Jesus, make it make sense.

Although I was determined to end things with Langston, I couldn't be sure if my heart fully agreed with my mind. His charm and understanding of me posed a constant challenge. Nonetheless, I stood prepared to finally end this emotional tug of war.

Langston and I sat across from each other in a cozy booth at a southern-style restaurant on Auburn Avenue. The tantalizing aroma of fried chicken, collard greens, black-eyed peas, macaroni and cheese, corn on the cob, fried green tomatoes, chitterlings and homemade cakes and pies overwhelmed our senses. The smell alone was enough to put anyone in a diabetic coma.

Our waitress, Ms. Mattie, was a sweet elderly woman donning a salt-and-pepper-colored wig with a hair net that had seen its glory far too many times. She greeted us with a bright orange apron that had a blend of flour and grease stains splattered on it, worn over a crisp white uniform, complete with white pantyhose and nursing-type shoes below with her swollen ankles peeled over them.

As she carefully poured water into two glasses on the table, I couldn't help but catch a whiff of Avon Skin So Soft lingering on her body amidst the scent of fried chicken. She was a beautiful woman in her mid to late seventies with a complexion the color of molasses. She had a beautiful smile that could light up a room and spoke with a heavy southern drawl.

She graciously asked, "May I take your order?"

I politely declined, and she asked, "You sure, baby?"

Langston looked up at me to see my response.

"Yes, I'm fine." Meanwhile, he ordered a bowl of gumbo, hot water cornbread, and a glass of sweet tea.

As he held my hands, we exchanged smiles, and my heart fluttered at his soft touch.

"How are you feeling?" he asked, adding, "You look beautiful, by the way," as he scanned my entire body.

"I'm doing okay. Some days are better than most."

"How are your friends?"

"It's been rough for all of us. Thanks for asking."

He nodded and said, "You bet."

Before I could say anything else, Ms. Mattie, with a slight limp, brought out a plate of gumbo with white rice buried underneath from the kitchen. All of the staff, including the cashier, were around seventy and over.

Langston, in his Southside Chicago accent, asked, "You feeling alright, Ms. Mattie?"

She nodded. "I'm just tired, baby."

"You need to take it easy."

"I know my kids want me to retire, but I want to work," she said with a hearty smoker's laugh. Ms. Mattie glanced over at me with a radiant smile adorned by a gleaming gold crown on her upper left tooth.

Langston had a way of making everyone around him feel special. Since his freshman year, he had been a loyal customer of this restaurant, and over time, the staff had become his extended family.

When the city posed a threat of shutting down the establishment due to unpaid property taxes, Langston took action. He reached out to the civil rights leaders within the community and alerted the media. As news spread about the potential closure of the seventy-five-year-old restaurant where King and Abernathy organized the movement, an anonymous wealthy donor stepped in to save the day.

On a few occasions, Langston gave Ms. Mattie a ride home when the weather was particularly bad. There was no specific reason behind his actions; he simply did them out of kindness.

The way he viewed the world was different and unique. He was beyond his years and would literally give the shirt off his back to a person in need. It was one of the many qualities that led me to fall in love with him. Langston possessed an old soul that I greatly admired.

The rain started to come down heavily. So, I leaned back in my chair, gazing out the rain-drenched window, and allowed the sound of raindrops to lull me into a sense of calm. I finally found the courage to tell him how I was feeling.

"Langston, we can't get back together again. My life is with Malik."

"Are you sure that's what you want?"

"Yes. I've made up my mind." Tears began rolling down my face faster than I could blink. "If you love me, you'll let me go."

"So, basically, I'm being judged for something that took place when we were in our early twenties." There were tears perched in his eyes. I gently reached out and wiped away one that had fallen to Langston's cheek.

"I do love you, but sometimes love means making difficult choices," I said softly. "I have to follow what's best for me, and that's Malik. He makes me feel alive, supported, and loved in a way that I've never experienced before. Besides, I want a family. I want to be a mom one day, and I don't want to miss that window of opportunity just so you can prolong this to suit your needs. I want to see how far this could go with Malik."

Langston nodded. His expression was a mix of sadness and a bit of frustration. "I just hope you'll be happy, even if it's not with me."

"I hope the same for you, Langston. You deserve to find someone who can give you the love and happiness you're looking for, too. But for now, we need to say goodbye."

The rain had finally stopped, which was a signal that it was time to go. We said our goodbyes, and I hurried out, leaping over a few puddles before entering my car.

I couldn't help but feel a sense of relief that it was over between Langston and me, but at the same time, I was overwhelmed. I cried to and from the grocery store. I debated whether I should finally tell Malik, but a part of me felt it wasn't necessary and that it was time to move on and focus on my relationship with Malik.

When I arrived home, he was multitasking, cooking dinner and drinking a Heincken while engrossed in his laptop. He had on a gray North Carolina A&T black hoodie.

I unpacked the grocery bag of breakfast items and stored them away for the morning. The familiar scent of Costa Rica filled the entire house, but missing was the smell of the ocean nearby, the alluring tropical flowers and delightful fruits. I so longed to get back to Costa Rica. It was home for me, and I missed Maverick and our daily strolls to and from the beach.

"Hey, babe. It smells good in here."

He leaned over and kissed me on the lips. "I'm finishing up this proposal. What do you think about us leaving Atlanta after Roxanne's wedding?"

"Babe, I am so ready to go home," I pleaded.

"Honey, just three more months."

Malik's business was expanding, and the new year held great promise. With Costa Rica being just one of several accounts, he felt that he didn't have to be so hands-on with Costa Rica since most of their initiatives proved to be working. Another worry was his mom's health, but that was stable now, too, with her diabetes controlled by insulin and a carefully regulated diet.

"Sure," I said hesitantly.

"We're working on one of our biggest projects to date, and I believe we have a good chance of being granted this contract."

"Well, staying a few extra months would allow me to spend more time with Elena's children," I added.

He smiled. "You see? Everything will fall into place," he assured me.

I took a nap in an attempt to erase the anxiety of emotions that transpired between Langston and me today. While I knew I did the right thing, it seemed like everything was crashing all at once, and I was trying my best to hold it all together.

I slept for a few hours when I woke up to familiar sounds of a dog panting and footsteps running up the stairwell leading to the bedrooms. I sat up and shouted, "Maverick!"

Malik opened the bedroom door, and Maverick came rushing into the room and jumped on my bed, where he licked my face over and over again. He was twice the size from when I saw him last. I began sobbing. My faithful companion and his unexpected arrival were the best surprises I could have ever asked for. I learned that Malik had coordinated Maverick's travel a month ago.

I spent the rest of the day cuddling, playing, and catching up with Maverick. Inspecting his body and teeth like a true mama with her child who's been away from her for too long.

While Malik focused on his report, Maverick and I went on a long walk and simply enjoyed each other's company. It felt as if we hadn't missed a beat, and our bond remained as strong as ever.

***

It had been a few weeks since the girls and I had seen each other. With the exception of an occasional group text message from time to time, we were all too busy with our personal lives to even meet up for brunch, our favorite pastime.

When Greg reached out to us about picking up boxes that Elena wanted us to have, suddenly, everyone found the time. I was too elated to even complain about us not getting together sooner.

When we pulled up to Elena's house, the chatter between us stopped as we mentally prepared ourselves for what lay ahead.

Camille greeted us at the door wearing a necklace that Greg had gifted Elena on their fifth wedding anniversary. The heart pendant with pink encrusted diamonds, custom-designed for Elena, caught my attention immediately, but I avoided drawing any attention to it for the sake of the others.

I reached out and hugged Camille. The others politely said hello and quickly walked past her to avoid any small talk. If that wasn't enough, the atmosphere was so different inside the house. In fact, the entire house looked nothing like before.

This million-dollar home, once Greg and Elena's forever home, was built from the ground up and furnished by one of Atlanta's premier black interior designers. Now, long gone, was any remnant of Elena's exquisite taste. It looked more like a step above a trailer park, with cheap art meant for a dentist's office.

The kids weren't around. Camille told us they were with Greg on a grocery run, and they would be back shortly.

As we followed Camille through the house, we took in room after room that once reflected elegance and sophistication.

Elena's former bedroom was now unofficially a storage room. Boxes were everywhere, piled against the walls. The house was cluttered and disorganized, a far cry from its former glory. Camille, sensing our confusion, apologized for the state of the house and explained that she had been too overwhelmed with grading her student papers and chaperoning the children to and from their extra-curricular activities to maintain the same level of care and attention. Greg offered to hire a nanny part-time. She sighed heavily, her shoulders slumping as though she was carrying the weight of the world. It was at that moment that we decided that we were not going to stay to open the boxes as we had initially planned.

"Elena marked the boxes of clothing that she wanted donated to a women's homeless shelter. Your boxes are right over there, and Elena left a note for each of you inside your boxes," Camille said awkwardly as she pointed. We each picked up a box with our name on it.

"Are you guys leaving?" Camille asked. "Greg and the kids should be heading back to the house soon."

I hugged Camille as we said goodbye. Hannah practically ran to her car.

"Keep in touch, Camille. Let me know if you need anything," I said.

As we rode home, there was a definite shift in mood between us. Hannah seemed irritated, tapping the steering wheel with her freshly manicured nails as though her nails were speaking for her. Flipping her freshly silk-pressed hair at heated moments, Roxanne remained silent as she usually does when she is in deep thought, staring out of the passenger window.

Curious about the boxes, I asked, "What do you think is in them?"

Hannah ignored my question and dialed Mike instead. Mike's voice came through the car speaker as he answered her call. "Hey," he said.

"Hey baby, I'm on my way home. I'll see you in a few," Hannah replied. After disconnecting the call, she blurted, "Did you see the condition of the home? Elena must be rolling in her grave."

"Camille's complaining was irritating me," Roxanne added. "Did she forget that she signed up for this?"

Hannah scoffed. "The job was never meant for her in the first place. That's what happens when you have no business stealing someone else's husband. I want to know why they were so damn quick to paint the house over? Elena hasn't been dead that long."

"Did you notice how she had on Elena's necklace?" I asked.

Roxanne quickly turned her face toward me in disbelief. "No, I didn't notice and Thank God, I didn't because I would've told her what's really on my mind."

Hannah said, "I know you guys don't want to hear this, but as long as Camille and Greg are together, she'll be involved with the kids. We'll have to interact with her. Besides, we promised Elena that we would remain in her children's lives."

"We know already. It's so hard for me, and I'm trying my best to stay strong."

Hannah broke down crying. "This shit is too much. I don't know if I'm going or if I'm coming. This is so unfair."

We all were so desperately trying to pick up the pieces, but coping with the loss of Elena was tougher than we all ever imagined. Grief weighed heavily on our hearts and minds.

There were mornings that even I couldn't get up and didn't know what to do with my life. Each day was a struggle for me, filled with a nagging emptiness that seemed impossible to shake. I wasn't ready to open up those feelings and Elena's box stayed in the closet.

Chapter 17

The Best Man

Malik was under a lot of stress from work, and it was gradually taking its toll on our relationship. I was craving his touch and his undivided attention.

I had never seen him this anxious before. After spending the entire day at the office, he would return home only to get caught up in more work calls and emails, sometimes late into the night.

I supported him as best as I could. I cooked dinner mostly every night and even ran his bath water for him, but Malik was hyper-focused and rarely acknowledged my efforts. He believed that if his agency didn't garner the contract they were vying for, it somehow reflected poorly on him. This was despite the numerous accolades his agency had received over the years from the international community and even The White House.

For some reason, I internalized the idea that maybe I was the root of the problem. It felt like he had built a wall around his emotions, leaving me feeling disconnected. I longed for him to open up to me more so I could help bridge this emotional divide between us, but he seemed so preoccupied and lost in his own thoughts that I was unsure about even approaching him.

Despite his assurance that I hadn't done anything wrong, I still struggled when he was silent. My mind always drifted back to Langston, recalling moments of our instant connection and understanding. While Malik is a tower of confidence in every aspect of his life, there is a slight insecurity that occasionally seeped above the surface and wreaked havoc on his emotions.

He was super hard on himself. No matter how much he projected self-confidence, a nagging doubt forever lingered in the back of his mind.

For Malik, his success wasn't just about his own personal achievement; it was about inspiring others. He took this role very seriously, often neglecting his own self-care at times.

There were a few black-owned environmental agencies throughout the country, and they all knew and supported one another—a win for one was a win for everyone, Malik often boasted.

I gave him the space he wanted, but I also made sure that he knew I was there for him if he needed me. It wasn't uncommon for me to ask him about his progress.

"Honey, is everything okay?

"Yes, everything is fine," he replied as he zeroed in on his laptop screen, clearly agitated about something.

"Babe, do you have a moment to talk?"

"What is it?" he yelled. I gave him a death stare and ran upstairs to the bedroom, and as he came running up behind me, he said, "Baby, I'm sorry. You have my attention now."

Maverick came running behind Malik and hopped on my bed. It appeared that he, too, was craving attention from Malik and wanted his belly rubbed.

Malik lay across the bed while I looked away in disgust, and he pleaded with me to talk to him.

I turned around and asked, "What is wrong with you? You haven't been yourself in a while. You come in, and you hardly say anything to me."

"I'm trying to get some work done."

"I feel like you're shutting me out."

"No, I'm just trying to get some work done."

"So, now I'm getting in the way of you getting your work done?"

"You know that I hate for you to see this part of me," he said, appearing embarrassed.

"What do you mean?"

"I've been like this since I was a kid. When I'm feeling overwhelmed, I block everyone out."

"Is that the best you can come up with?"

Malik sighed. "Babe, my sister and I grew up believing mediocrity was a bad word. It was reinforced in us that we hailed from kings and queens and there was nothing we couldn't do if we put our minds to doing it. Sadly, we also learned that we had to work twice as hard to gain half as much."

"Well, guess what? I was told the same thing. My Central American parents drilled it in us. If I came home with an A-minus, my parents would ask me what happened and why I didn't earn a solid A instead of rewarding me. While most kids slept in on Saturdays, my sister and I were in the library bright and early studying. Stop being so hard on yourself. Your agency is more than qualified and deserving to manage this account."

"I'm working on doing better."

"So where do I fit in?"

"What do you mean? I can't read your mind, Tiff. You haven't said much either."

"Are you serious right now?"

"I know you're still hurting over Elena's death."

"Please don't expect me to be okay after a month."

"I know it's a lot to process, so I thought I would step back a little bit."

"Don't think for me. Ask me what I need, and don't assume. Listen, if loving me is too much for you, let me know."

"Tiff, there's no question that I can handle what we have here. I love you, and I chose you to be in my life."

He took my hands and pulled me toward him and held me in his arms. A part of me was afraid I would lose him.

"Stop crying, babe. Everything is going to be fine with us."

I lifted my head and asked, "Are you sure?"

"Yes. And I'm sorry for raising my voice. I'll do better next time."

"You better."

I was relieved that we were able to sort things out. At least for now. After a little snuggling time, I decided to take Maverick for a walk. Malik had never raised his voice with me before, and I needed time to clear my head and take everything in. He offered to come along, and I said no. I told him to focus on his work.

***

It was a surreal moment, and I couldn't believe it was actually happening. My bestie Roxanne was trying on wedding dresses.

The luxurious bridal boutique with grand Sikorsky Crystal chandeliers hanging above us and love ballads playing in the background presented a scene taken from a fairytale. A collection of elegant wedding gowns to choose from surrounded us, hanging in a range of styles, sectioned off by the designers.

Glasses of champagne were graciously handed to each of us by the attendants while Roxanne slipped into different wedding gowns and modeled for us. With each new gown Roxanne tried on, the room filled with tears of joy, particularly from Dr. Janice.

Roxanne's mom and her crew were a feisty bunch, all of whom were members of Alpha Kappa Alpha Sorority Inc., medical doctors and classmates at Bennett College. As Dr. Janice liked to remind everyone, Bennett College is the real sister college for Morehouse.

It was striking how Roxanne and her mother looked so much alike. Dr. Janice, a former Jet Beauty in 1979, had a whirlwind romance with Muhammad Ali, a fact she frequently boasted about. She had hazel eyes, a tawny complexion and freckles that sprinkled perfectly above her cheeks, and her auburn hair, now touched with gray roots, fell to her shoulders. Despite being sixty-three years old, she still maintained her infamous hourglass figure that left men in awe.

After spending nearly two hours watching Roxanne try on different styles of wedding gowns, she finally emerged in one that left everyone in the room speechless. Overwhelmed with emotion, Roxanne burst into tears. "Mommy, this is the one."

"Yes, baby. You've found it," replied Dr. Janice. Not a single person in the room had a dry eye.

***

The day had finally arrived, and I was still a little hungover from two nights ago from the bachelorette party. Roxanne was adamant about not having strippers—she couldn't trust how her mama and aunties would act while under the influence of alcohol. Plus, Roxanne invited a few of her colleagues and didn't want to be embarrassed by her mom, who hooked up with one of the strippers at her cousin's bachelorette party a few years ago.

Dr. Janice said, "That young man brought back twenty years of my life."

Despite no strippers, we all managed to have a good time. The groomsman, on the other hand, hosted a bachelor party at Magic

City. Everyone, including Malik, was tight-lipped on what actually took place that night. All I knew was that Malik's hard penis woke me up at 4:00 AM.

Roxanne's bridal party enjoyed the luxury of having a suite to ourselves, complete with a professional glam squad that included nail technicians, makeup artists, and hairstylists. We even had massages. Our elegant one-shoulder dusty-rose bridesmaids' dresses beautifully complemented the varying shades of melanin within the bridal party and accentuated our curves. Our hair was styled in sleek, pulled-back ponytails with a side sweep.

As we lined up to enter the church, Hannah led the way. When she reached the front to join the other bridesmaids, she was visibly emotional, holding back tears.

When Roxanne walked in with her dad, the reaction on Scott's face fighting back the tears was priceless. Roxanne looked beautiful, wearing a designer satin sleeveless dress with a three-dimensional lace floral embroidery that wrapped around her entire gown. Her ringlet curls lay perfectly past her shoulders.

My bridal partner Tim, Scott's roommate from college, and I made our way down the aisle. I saw Malik pointing his cell phone in our direction.

When I looked to my immediate left, I saw Langston. Our eyes met across the crowded room, and memories of our past began flooding back to me. I felt like I was stuck in some sort of time capsule and had nowhere to escape.

I held my composure, and I squeezed Tim's hand tightly as we strolled down the aisle and waved to the guests. I couldn't believe Langston was here and with a date. I was feeling anxious as we exchanged forced smiles, and I tried to avoid any interaction between us.

***

Hannah and I delivered our wedding toasts, and emotions ran high as I mentioned Elena's presence and felt a surge of love. Hannah raised her glass and expressed wishes for a lifetime of love while I tried to hold back my tears. As we all clinked our glasses and savored our champagne, Roxanne and Scott couldn't keep their hands off of each other.

After Roxanne and Scott had their first dance, the DJ welcomed the entire bridal party to join them. I held Tim's hand as we swayed with the other couples to Rascal Flatts' "Bless the Broken Road."

Despite trying to discreetly scan the room, Tim's tall and wide stature blocked any chances of me spotting Langston in the crowded and dimly lit reception hall.

Midway through the dance, Malik tapped Tim's shoulder and gestured that he would take over as more couples joined in on the dancing. We slow danced to a couple of songs. Malik was tipsy, his breath smelling of brown liquor, and his bravado was on ten as he held on to me tightly.

Hannah and Mike were locking lips at every chance they could get and even slowed dance while everyone was engrossed in learning the new Beyoncé inspired line dance.

Greg was getting his groove on with a woman who eerily looked like Elena. This came on the heels of his announcement made at the bachelor party that he'd ended his relationship with Camille and that she had moved out.

Greg didn't go into detail as to why they broke up, but he did talk about their arrangement. She had the kids two days out of the week and two weekends out of the month. I wasn't surprised, but I was relieved that she kept her promise to Elena.

Langston and his date were dancing nearby, and there were a few awkward moments where our eyes met. Dr. Janice was slow dancing with someone's thirty-something-year-old grandson while Roxanne's dad stayed at the bar drinking tequila shots.

As the waitstaff began serving the cake, I made a run to the ladies' room, where I bumped into Langston, of all people, leaving the men's room.

I was like a deer in headlights, as I couldn't believe he was standing right in front of me. We both looked around to see if anyone was watching and then he pulled me into a utility room adjacent to the restrooms.

Before I could react, the door swung shut behind us, locking us inside. I yanked on the door a few times, but it wouldn't open. *Great*, I thought. *How in the world am I going to explain this to Malik?*

In the confined space, silence came between us as we tried to register the awkward situation we found ourselves in.

Breaking the silence, I finally spoke up. "Why did you pull me in here? Langston, Malik is probably looking for me."

"Who would've thought we'd end up locked in a closet together?"

I nodded. "Yeah, talk about a twist of fate. It's been a while since we've seen each other, and now we're trapped in a closet."

We both laughed, breaking the tension that had been building.

Langston didn't stop staring at me. "Damn, baby, you look good! Turn around for me."

Langston, stop."

"Come on, baby."

I began to blush as I turned around in the tight space. "Look," I began, but before I could finish, he pulled me toward him and began kissing me passionately.

I pulled away. "I can't do this with you, Langston. What is it that you don't seem to understand? I love Malik. Now, get me out of here before I start screaming."

I began knocking on the door, and Langston pressed in from behind me. "You know you miss me," he whispered. He began removing my dress, and I couldn't resist, so I unbuttoned his shirt and pulled his tie off as he unzipped his pants. They fell to his ankles, exposing his dress socks and ashy legs.

He lifted me up as my legs wrapped around his waist. Every time he entered me, I closed my eyes in sheer ecstasy as I listened to him moan, and I cried out his name. He whispered how much he missed me and how much he loved me.

We made love for what seemed like forever. Langston removed some tablecloths that were on a shelf and placed them on the floor, where we sat cuddled together. I took some napkins from my purse and wiped his brow.

Outside the janitor's closet, the wedding continued, blissfully unaware of what had transpired between Langston and me.

Once we got dressed, we both began knocking on the door, hoping someone would hear us. I had two missed calls from Malik, and Langston had several text messages from his date questioning his whereabouts.

Eventually, a staff person heard us knocking and opened the door. As the door was opened, we stepped out with what I'm sure was *oh shit, we've been caught* expressions written all over our faces.

The staffer chuckled as we tried to compose ourselves, and Langston and I returned to our seats with our respective partners, the two of us acting as though nothing happened. The rest of the wedding unfolded without any further unexpected surprises.

Chapter 18

Trading Places

Camille and I arranged to meet for coffee. When she entered Starbucks, I sat near a large bay window, people-watching and catching up on work emails.

She wore fitted denim jeans and a Stella McCartney coral crop sweater top that came directly from Elena's closet. Her shoulder-length hair had a lot of body, unlike its usual lifeless appearance. This visible transformation was different. Nonetheless, it was evident that she was in a much happier space.

Camille wasted no time and dived right into discussing the reasons behind her breakup with Greg. She assumed I knew, and I did, but I didn't want her to know that.

Instead, I tried changing the subject a few times, but she cleverly steered the conversation back to Greg again and again. It seemed she was determined to set the record straight. While I was curious to know her side of the story, part of me wanted no part of it. Besides, I was dealing with my own drama, and I had no intention of becoming a relationship advisor for someone else.

"How are the children coping with you moving out?" I asked.

"It's been particularly challenging for both of them, especially for Kniya," she shared. "She's very close to me and is still struggling with the loss of her mother. She's experiencing separation anxiety, feeling as though she may have done something wrong and having difficulty understanding why we can't all live together."

I didn't interrupt her and only nodded as she continued.

"Greg and I have explained to the kids that he needs to work, which is why they spend two nights with me during the week. On Kniya's birthday, we played a video of Elena, thinking it would make her feel better, but that only resulted in her crying uncontrollably. The therapist advised us to delay sharing more videos until the kids are older and better equipped to process them."

Camille paused before adding, "Are you aware that Greg was seeing multiple women while he was married to Elena?"

"Does that really matter?"

"Well, he's not the man he claimed to be."

"To who? You?"

Camille had a puzzled look on her face and I got the impression she wasn't quite sure how to handle my sudden shift in attitude. "I hope I haven't offended you in any way."

"Greg cheated on his wife with you, so it doesn't surprise me to know there were others."

I knew not to ask her if there was any chance of them reconciling, especially after witnessing him grinding on his date at the wedding.

An awkward silence between us followed. Camille's alabaster cheeks were now flushed with hues of red and pink, and then she began to cry as she expressed more of her feelings.

"I grew to love Elena and never intended to cause her any pain."

"Well, thank you for keeping your promise to Elena. I'm grateful for everything you've done."

"I love her children."

"I know you do." I could sense her sincerity, and after that exchange, she quickly changed the subject.

"How's Malik?"

"He's fine." I looked down at my watch. "Well, speaking of which, I need to get going."

"When are you guys traveling back to Costa Rica?"

"Malik's agency was awarded a new contract here in Atlanta. It's his biggest project to date, and it appears we'll be around until mid-summer, no later than the fall."

Camille nodded. "Well, thank you for offering to meet with me."

"Let's set up a date with the kids," I said.

"Yes, for sure."

"I'll be in touch."

***

Another trip around the sun, I thought to myself this morning as Malik wished me a happy birthday before leaving for the office. He made dinner plans for us that evening, but I said I would prefer we spend the day together.

He handed me a card with five one-hundred-dollar bills and a dozen roses. He suggested I treat myself to a massage.

Hannah sent me a text message letting me know that she couldn't hang out with me because she was hosting a special news broadcast on the local elections. And Roxanne and Scott weren't expected to return from their honeymoon until later that night.

Instead of wallowing in pity, I took the day off and did some retail therapy. I made time for a leisurely lunch and headed off to the salon afterward to enjoy a facial and massage, as Malik suggested. I wanted to look extra special tonight for him.

Langston called while I was under the hair dryer to wish me a happy birthday and said he wanted to see me. I told him no and that I had plans with Malik.

Ever since our last encounter, Langston had been like a nagging fly that kept trying to buzz his way back into my life even though I continually swatted him away.

With the exception of having to occasionally yell over bachata music, Carmen did an excellent job styling my hair, which cascaded down to the arch of my back.

Carmen was a beautiful trans woman from DR who could really do some hair. She was petite with long flowing hair and a beautiful olive complexion. She spoke with a heavy accent.

She had been doing my hair off and on for years, and whenever I was in town, and I wanted a Dominican blowout, I made sure to be in her seat, although I made sure to bring my own shampoo and conditioner, specially ordered from my go-to salon in Washington Heights. I wanted to avoid any potential issues with the shampoo girl accidentally using chemicals on my natural hair, so I came prepared with my own products.

Carmen and I played catch-up. I told her about Malik. She told me about her husband and how they adopted her sister's kids. She said she loved being a mom to those kids.

Carmen asked to see a photo of Malik, and after she was done with my hair, she escorted me to the back of her salon. We sat across from each other as she began speaking in Spanish, while she took sips of rum and held a rosary in her hand. There were candles and religious statuettes all around the room. She pulled out a deck of tarot cards and placed them one by one on the table.

She asked me to place his photo on the table then spoke in Spanish again and also in English, assuring me that Malik is a good man and that he loved me. She also saw another man in the picture who she sensed could potentially cause problems in my relationship.

"Girlfriend, you got to choose one man. They both have strong feelings for you."

I was skeptical when it came to psychic readers, but she knew exactly what I had been feeling.

I left the salon feeling torn, as I've expressed to Langston that it was over many times, and yet we still manage to see each other. The last thing I wanted to do was hurt Malik with this back-and-forth with Langston.

***

Malik and I celebrated my birthday at our favorite Brazilian restaurant known for its succulent meat. Shortly before arriving, Malik made it perfectly clear that he wanted to go home after dinner to catch the remainder of the Warriors game against the Lakers.

Throughout dinner, he kept resorting to staring at his cell phone to keep tabs on the score while also responding to work-related text messages. He'd dressed in acid-washed oversized denim jeans, a throwback Warren Moon football jersey, and a du-rag that was worn tightly on his head. It was enough for anyone to mistake him for a broke college student.

I whispered, "Babe, take your du-rag off." He quickly pulled it off and placed his hands under the table.

It wasn't like him to dress this way, not to mention on a special occasion like my birthday. On top of that, he didn't even notice that my hair was styled differently. He'd only seen my hair straight and free of my coils maybe twice since we'd been together, and I thought it would grab his attention.

Things were getting weird between us, but I was trying to make the best of our evening. Besides, I couldn't remember the last time we went out on a date.

I wanted to check out a movie after dinner, but Malik insisted again that he was going home to watch the remainder of the basketball game. I was annoyed, but I just went along with his plans and asked the waitress to provide me with a to-go box.

The ride back home was quiet. My thoughts were all over the place, and even though he tried to get my attention and was being playful with me by leaning over to kiss me several times, I was not in the mood. At this point, all I wanted to do was get home, shower and act like this night never happened.

When we pulled up to the house, I noticed there were several cars parked in front of my neighbor's home. As I was about to leave the car, another text message alert rang on Malik's phone. I was impatient, and I exited the car while Malik stayed behind to reply.

Malik called me back, and I just ignored him and hurriedly walked away. I'd had enough of him constantly on his damn cell phone. It was rude and downright disrespectful.

As I placed the key in the door, Malik came running up behind me. When I opened the door and flicked on the lights, I was startled when I heard voices from a group of familiar faces yelling, "Surprise!"

I was so overwhelmed with emotion that I turned to Malik and hugged him tightly, a flood of tears streaming down my face while he whispered he loved me.

The night was an absolute blast. I couldn't remember the last time I laughed and danced so much. Scott and Roxanne had just returned from their honeymoon, appearing a few hues darker than when they left, well-rested and in love. Hannah, Mike, and a bunch of other close friends gathered to celebrate my birthday too.

We danced to some of my favorite tunes from the early 2000s, with the theme of the party designating a throwback to apartment CC-4, which explained Malik's outfit and du-rag.

Everyone was decked out in baggy denim jeans, flannel shirts, and bra tops, channeling that iconic 2000-era look.

Red cups were filled with drinks as we grooved to some classic hits from back in the day. We even had a lively soul train line that kept us dancing for what felt like hours.

As the night wound down, the guys made their way to the back of the house for bourbon and cigars while the ladies and I gathered around the kitchen island.

Half-empty bowls of chips, red and green salsa, and guacamole surrounded us, remnants of a night well spent. I wanted to fill the girls in on how I was feeling lately, but I didn't want to ruin the mood, so I sat back and listened to Roxanne recount her romantic honeymoon with Scott. Even if I had wanted to express myself, she was dominating the conversation and not giving anyone else a chance to speak.

Hannah and I were all ears listening intently as Roxanne described everything from the bed linen thread count to the jacuzzi in her luxurious hotel room suite. Though I had never seen her this happy, I surely didn't want to ruin her moment with tales of how I had sex with my ex in a closet at her wedding.

***

"Hey, babe, wake up." Malik's soothing voice managed to ease through my drowsiness. I blinked myself awake and saw him standing by the bed, holding a tray full of breakfast food. The aroma of bacon, buttery syrup-drenched pancakes, and coffee permeated the room. Maverick hopped onto the bed, his tail wagging, eyeing the food.

"Good morning," Malik said, planting a kiss on my forehead.

"You didn't have to make breakfast," I murmured.

"Anything for you, baby," he replied with a smile.

"Thank you, love." I rubbed my temples, trying to ease the pounding headache. The last conversation from the night before that I could remember was Roxanne announcing that she and Scott were heading home to "make a baby." The rest was a blur, lost to fatigue and tequila.

I didn't have much of an appetite, so I took a couple of bites of the food and fed the rest to Maverick. After I showered, I joined

Malik downstairs and helped him clean up from the party, but something seemed off with him. The pensive look on his face was a dead giveaway that he had something on his mind. I wondered what caused his mood to suddenly change.

"Honey, are you okay? What's wrong?"

"Who the fuck is Langston?" he shouted.

"Langston?" I echoed.

"Yes. Who is he?"

In an instant, a lump formed in my throat, making it impossible for me to breathe, let alone speak. My world seemed to crumble around me, leaving me uncertain of what to do next, so it took me a minute to muster the courage.

"Why do you ask?"

"I've heard his name thrown around a few times among the guys. A few nights ago, you called out his name in your sleep. Not once, but twice. Tiff, I need some answers, like right now."

"Okay. Okay, so Langston is my ex from college."

"Wait. The dude who was at the bachelor party and at the wedding? I think I even saw him at Elena's funeral. You never said anything." He narrowed his eyes. "Wait a minute. Did you fuck him?"

Before I could say a word, my face said it all. The guilt was too much to hide.

"Damn, Tiff! How could you?" he yelled as he pounded his fist on the table. "Don't you know I love you? What we have here is real to me. I'm building a future for us, for our family. I've been shopping around town looking for the perfect ring. You got me looking like a damn fool."

"Malik, I'm so sorry," I cried, tears and snot running down my face so intensely that my eyelashes clung to my cheeks. "I never wanted to hurt you. Please, please forgive me," I pleaded, reaching for his hand, but he pulled it away sharply.

"You love that nigga?"

I hesitated.

"Answer me now," he demanded.

"I don't know."

"You don't know?" He chuckled. "Fuck this. I'm out of here."

"Wait, baby," I pleaded.

"Tiff, I can't do this with you anymore. I need to be left alone," he shouted, snatching his keys from the table and slamming the door behind him.

I fell to the ground, overwhelmed by the pain of losing him, and as Malik's tires screeched away, the echo of him leaving nearly killed me.

I spent most of the night curled up on the floor near the door in a fetal position, waiting for him with Maverick by my side, offering comfort.

Malik didn't return, and anxiety gnawed at me, fearing the worst, until a text from him shattered any hope. He wanted me out of the house; he needed space.

I tried to call him repeatedly, but he wouldn't pick up. When I insisted that we talk, his response was final—our relationship was over.

Chapter 19

Dream Girls

The house was in virtual silence as Roxanne, Hannah and I formed an assembly line and began passing my clothes and shoes from the closet into boxes, along with other items I'd accumulated since being in Atlanta.

"These are cute," Hannah remarked.

"Oh, thanks. I got those on sale at Nordstrom's Rack," I replied.

Reluctant to betray their men, both were tight-lipped about sharing too much of Malik's side of the story, so I only caught fragments of it. However, eventually, Hannah, aka CNN, couldn't hold back any longer, and she spilled all the tea.

As she handed me a pair of boots, she whispered, "You know, he's been saying some things that don't add up. Girl, to be honest with you, I never thought he was good for you in the first place."

This was news to me that she didn't like him for me.

"He's painting you in a bad light," she added, "and I think it's only fair that you know." She looked over at Roxanne for a reaction.

I paused, holding the boot in mid-air, processing her words. The air felt thick with tension as Roxanne avoided eye contact, focusing intently on neatly folding a sweater. I knew then that this packing party planned by Hannah was more than just helping me move out—it was about uncovering truths and deciding where loyalties should lay.

"Were you cheating on him with Langston?" Hannah asked. "That's what the streets are saying."

So, I finally broke down and told them everything about my affair with Langston.

Hannah carefully weighed every word I spoke, staring at me as if she were a human lie detector, scrutinizing every expression and pause between my words.

As I confessed, the tears began falling. "I had no desire to be with anyone else. But after we ran into each other at the nightclub, and he later contacted me through LinkedIn, Langston's persistence made it difficult. I tried to break it off with him several times, but the more I said no, the more he refused to stop contacting me. I felt trapped and conflicted," I admitted between sobs.

"Langston saw me in a way that Malik didn't. And Langston was my first love. We have history together. I mean, it's no excuse, but at times, I felt so alone, and so I got caught up in Langston's world."

The atmosphere was intense with my confession, and for a long moment, neither Hannah nor Roxanne spoke. They both sat quietly, cross-legged on the carpet, absorbing the weight of my words, surrounded by Maverick, empty boxes, and piles of clothes and shoes.

"Would you consider dating Langston again?" Hannah finally asked.

"I can't think about that right now," I responded quietly. I really wanted to say hell no, but I was too ashamed to admit that Langston ghosted me after my breakup with Malik. We made plans to meet up twice, and he never showed. I even went by the diner, and they hadn't seen him in months.

Roxanne said, "Well, Langston doesn't give me the impression that he wants to be tied down anyway."

I wondered what Roxanne knew that she wasn't sharing. But I wasn't too concerned. Hannah would likely get it out of her, and then she'd come running to me and swear me to secrecy.

The dynamic of our friendship was complicated. It went back to college. In moments like these, I was reminded of the strange comfort in knowing that no secret stayed hidden for long among us.

***

With most of my belongings shipped off, I was close to being ready to leave for Costa Rica. I informed Malik that I would be gone at the end of the month.

We occasionally ran into each other at the house, usually when he was picking up his mail or stopped by for a change of clothes. We hardly spoke during these brief encounters.

A few times, I caught him staring at my ass. Each time our eyes met, he would abruptly turn away, adding an unspoken tension to our already strained interactions.

I lost my appetite, and the changes in me were becoming noticeable. My clothes were loose on me, bringing me down to the size I wore in high school, and it seemed he was grappling with his own set of problems. According to Hannah, Malik was crashing at her and Mike's house and sleeping on their couch.

I was sure that in Hannah's passive-aggressive way, she was giving Malik hell, and he was dying to be in his own space.

Despite everything that had happened between us, I missed him so much. I was so disappointed in myself for how I'd betrayed his trust. We were inseparable before all this, and the silence between us was driving me nuts. It was filled with all the words we hadn't said to each other, and with each passing day, the weight of our breakup began taking its toll on me.

I feared we would never get past this pain.

***

I dropped by Greg's place to visit the kids, and I found him in the kitchen making lunch. He was preparing Elena's signature grilled cheese on sourdough bread with Gruyère cheese and truffle butter, just as she used to make it. He'd also prepared homemade tomato soup, complete with fresh tomatoes and basil from her garden, one of the things he'd made sure to keep intact. On days like this, I really felt Elena's absence.

Greg Junior and Kniya were miniature-sized versions of their parents. Kniya was a talker and inquisitive like her mama, while Greg Junior didn't say much but was very observant.

After lunch, when the kids ran off to play in their rooms, Greg casually inquired about Malik. Before I could even answer, he mentioned hearing about our breakup.

"How are you holding up?" he asked.

I thought to myself, *does everyone in Atlanta already know?* It seemed Malik was now considered an eligible bachelor, soon to join Atlanta's dating pool.

Honestly, I didn't think my relationship with Greg was at a level where discussing my personal life felt appropriate. Sure, I may have stepped out on Malik, but I'm no serial cheater like Greg, so why is this even a topic of conversation? What advice could he possibly have that could salvage my relationship with Malik?

Greg obviously noticed my discomfort because he said, "I don't want to pry into your business."

"Then don't," I replied. "Anyway, I need to leave now. I have another appointment."

Then he dropped a bombshell. "I talked to Malik."

I gave him a *no this motherfucker didn't* look.

"I told him you're a good woman and said, 'Don't be like me. Do what you can to get her back in your life.'"

I was stunned. "Thank you, Greg." I smiled. "You didn't have to."

"It was the least I could do. Man, Malik is a good brother, and I hope you guys work things out."

Greg walked me out to the car and gave me a huge embrace. "I'll be in touch," I said as I waved goodbye.

***

When I pulled up to the house, Malik's car was parked in the driveway, and I immediately began to panic at the sight of his car. I was glad he was home, but our strained relationship made being around each other awkward. I stopped counting how many times I'd begged for his forgiveness.

Every time I brought up the idea of us working things out, he became easily agitated and dismissive. At times, I felt like he didn't know that I even existed, which made me question if he ever loved me at all.

"I guess our love isn't worth fighting for," I said to him during a heated argument.

He'd replied, "Maybe you need to ask yourself that."

I know I fucked up big time, but I never imagined our breakup would be so painful.

When I walked in, Malik and Maverick were curled up together on the couch. Maverick sprang out from under the blanket, his tail wagging furiously. He leaped off the couch, nearly toppling everything within reach.

Malik peeked out from under the covers, looking like he hadn't seen a barber in months. The table was cluttered with a bottle of

Tylenol, NyQuil, and crumpled used tissues, alongside his laptop and work papers.

He looked surprised to see me home, although I'm not sure why when I'd told him I wouldn't be gone until the end of the month.

Before I could ask him about his well-being, a beautiful woman emerged from the bathroom. The sight of her was a shock that hit me hard.

"Oh, hi. I'm Amanda," she said as she reached out to shake my hand. "I work with Malik. Are you Tiffany?"

"Yes. Nice to meet you."

"I've heard so many good things about you," she said with a smile. "Malik wasn't feeling well, so I offered to drive him home. My fiancé is nearby, so he's on his way to pick me up. She glanced at her cell phone when a car horn beeped. "That's him. Take care, Malik, and get some rest. We've got you covered at the office. Nice to meet you. Tiffany. See you at the gala," she added before leaving.

"Yes, for sure," I replied awkwardly.

Malik stood to explain as soon as the door closed behind her. "I was going to invite you to the ceremony, but I just hadn't gotten around to it. We've been swamped at the office, and—"

"Yeah, right." I grabbed my car keys and stormed out. I drove aimlessly around town until I was nearly out of gas. Eventually, hunger gnawed at me, so I swung by a nearby popular seafood boil takeout spot for a quick bite.

As I was entering the parking lot, my eyes caught sight of a man who looked like Langston. He was pushing a baby carriage and holding hands with a toddler, accompanied by a woman who held the child's other hand. I recognized the woman as his date at the wedding.

I couldn't believe what I was seeing and quickly snapped a picture with my cell phone. It was definitely Langston with a family that he never mentioned. I tried calling him to confront him about it, but it kept going straight to voicemail.

I parked my car and contemplated whether to approach him, but I decided not to. I sat in my car, hoping this was a nightmare that would end soon. How could Langston lie to me like that? He told me he loved me and wanted us to be together.

I was so fed up with deceitful ass men, and I was so ready to leave for Costa Rica.

I tried calling Roxanne to vent, but she was heading into a meeting. Fortunately, I managed to reach Hannah, who was anchoring the news. We occasionally texted each other during her newscast commercials, so I sent her a photo of Langston with his family.

"Who is that?" Hannah asked.

"Langston," I replied.

"Did he tell you he was married?"

"Of course not."

"That's not all I found out."

"What else?"

"Malik's co-worker told me about the awards ceremony."

"I thought you knew about it," she wrote. "Roxanne and Scott were also invited. Well, are you going to attend?"

"No. Why should I?"

"You are in love with him, right? Stop making this worse than it should be."

She went silent after that, which meant she was either frustrated or signing off on air for the night.

Chapter 20

Red Tails

I went to several boutiques but couldn't find anything that grabbed my attention. Most of my formal dresses had been shipped to Costa Rica. I was unsure about the mood between us—should I dress as Malik's date? He invited me to the awards gala but never mentioned if we were attending together.

I finally settled for a red, backless dress that reached down my ankles. It was a bit pricey, but anything that could get Malik's attention was worth the cost. I still had Hannah's gold Jimmy Choo shoes, and they paired perfectly with the dress.

Here I was, running late and wanting to get Malik's attention and impress his colleagues. I wondered if he would introduce me as his girlfriend or his ex. Still, I was excited. This was the first time Malik and I would be in public together since our breakup. *This should be interesting.*

I was escorted to Malik's table and sat across from Hannah and Mike. Scott and Roxanne were seated opposite me. When I glanced at Hannah, she seemed disappointed and looked away. I wondered if it was because of my outfit—was I showing too much of my back? Most of the attendees were uptight, nerdy engineers and scientists.

As I scanned the table for Malik, I saw him seated with a richly beautiful melanated woman with a low buzz haircut, high defined cheekbones and a mole that sat perfectly above her round lips. She was clearly his date.

Like art, she looked like she had fallen from the pages of *Vogue* and *Essence*. I shot him a dirty look, and I didn't care if everyone at the table noticed. He tried to introduce me, but I wanted no part of him.

Roxanne looked over at me and lifted her head as a gesture for me to do the same.

I couldn't believe Malik. How could he do this to me? Mostly, everyone around the table knew us as a couple. His staff members looked confused, including Amanda, the one I'd met the other day.

Embarrassed by their glances in my direction, I headed to the ladies' room, hoping to make some sense out of this foolishness, but then again, this was what I deserved, I told myself, unable to stop crying.

Hannah joined me in the bathroom and began gently powdering the area around my eyes to preserve what was left of my makeup.

"I can't believe Malik is acting like such an ass. I get that I did something wrong, and I make no excuse for my actions. But it's like he wants me to pay for the pain I caused him."

Roxanne walked into the bathroom then and immediately began examining her hair and makeup in the vanity mirror. "Girl, you are wearing the hell out of that dress," she said.

"Okay, Brickhouse." Hannah nodded in agreement.

"When you walked in, everyone looked at you," she added.

"I was afraid that maybe my dress was a bit risqué."

"No. You look amazing in it," Roxanne assured me.

"Malik didn't notice," I said sadly. "He was too busy talking to his date."

Hannah clicked her tongue. "Here's the scoop. Apparently, that's his on-and-off ex from many moons ago, and they're just friends."

Roxanne asked, "Why would he invite Tiffany and his ex to the same event? That's not cool."

I dabbed at my eyes. "Well, it didn't make me feel any better, and I'm ready to leave."

***

I was seething with anger, and I'd had enough of Malik and his bullshit. I stayed as long as I could, but Hannah's Jimmy Choo shoes were killing my feet. Besides, I couldn't bear to watch Malik and his date enjoying themselves any longer, so I left.

When I pulled into the driveway, I saw Malik's car. I thought to myself, *there's no way he could have reached here before me*. I know I was caught in traffic, but still. My mind began to race and I mentally couldn't catch up. Did he bring that woman home with him? My heart pounded with anxiety as I exited the car.

As soon as I got inside the house, I kicked off my shoes. I could hear movement from somewhere in the house, and seconds later, Malik opened the door, and Maverick ran toward me at full speed, practically knocking me down.

"We need to talk," Malik demanded.

"I have nothing to say to you." I walked right past him. He followed me to the bedroom, examining every inch of my body as I climbed the stairs, where I immediately stripped down to just a thong.

I threw on a T-shirt, descended the stairs, and poured myself a glass of wine. Then I passed out on the couch watching late-night TV.

Sometime later, I was awakened by Malik, who appeared to be eager to talk, but I couldn't make out a damn thing he was saying. I did hear him say "sorry" a few times and could tell he was drunk, but I was too tired to listen, so I rolled over on the couch. He slid right in beside me, and we fell asleep in each other's arms.

As dawn crept in, the sky began to fill with hues of pink and orange, casting a shadow of light on the wall and signaling Sunday had arrived.

Malik began gently rubbing my breast and pulling and sucking on my nipples. I woke up feeling extra warm and moist, so I gave in to those feelings.

He began to kiss me below, sticking his tongue in and out of my vagina and then resorted to placing his hard penis inside me.

It had been a while since Malik and I had been together intimately. My heart, body, and soul yearned for every inch of him, and I quivered every time he entered me.

I climbed on top of him as he adjusted his body to meet mine. My silk-pressed hair kept falling in my face as I bounced up and down, and each time, he would gently move strands of my hair to the side.

He cupped my breast and held on to my waist as I rode him until he came. We both nodded off to sleep and the next thing I remember, his hard penis pressed against my body again, sending shock waves that alerted me he wanted more.

He turned me over, and I grabbed hold of the couch's arm in a willful position while he moved his lower body inward and outward. When I climaxed, I screamed his name so loudly that Maverick ran into the room to assess the situation. He looked at us like, "Those two again?" and then turned and sat in his crate.

We both fell into laughter. "Ah, I miss my baby so much," Malik crooned.

"I've missed you too." I draped myself over his sweaty chest as he caressed my hair and kissed me dozens of times on my forehead and cheeks.

"Man, you had a nigga hard up in here," he exclaimed with extra bass in his voice, imitating actor and comedian Martin Lawrence. "I was going through bottles of lotion as if it was water. I think I've got carpal tunnel on my left hand," he added, and I couldn't stop laughing.

"What do you mean?" I asked coyly.

"You were walking around here in your Batty Rider," he said in Jamaican patois.

"What? Batty Rider?" Wait. Do you mean my booty shorts? I wear those when I'm cleaning."

"That's news to me."

"You've seen me wear those shorts before."

He made a face. "One morning, you sprayed your perfume, and I swear, my dick wouldn't go down. When you came out of the bedroom, I ran back into the bathroom."

"Is that why you slammed the door?"

"I thought you were trying to torture me."

We laughed and touched so much that it felt like we were little kids who couldn't get enough of each other.

"Babe, you are my best friend, and I miss spending time with you."

"What stopped you from speaking to me?" I asked.

"My ego got the best of me." He paused, then asked, "Are you in love with me, Tiff?"

I sat up and looked him directly in the face. "I never stopped loving you."

"Okay. Then what's the deal with you and Langston? And be honest."

"Nothing. Nothing at all. Plus, he's married."

"He's married? Did you know he was married?"

"Not until recently. Listen, I have no interest in him. I admit I was stupid and vulnerable, and it will never happen again. I promise you."

"I want to be able to trust you. I want you to only think of me—to only want to be with me. If there's a problem between us, tell me. This whole ordeal crushed me to my core. Some days, I felt like I couldn't go on without you."

"Malik, I never meant to hurt you. And I wish I could take that pain away. I was afraid you would never speak to me again."

"You know you're the best thing that has ever happened to me," he said, leaning in and kissing me. "I know I was focused on work, but I'm learning I need to balance things out. The work will get done."

"Please don't blame yourself. I was wrong for stepping out on our relationship. You've been so good to me. Since Elena died, I just don't know what to do with myself. I hate my job, but I make extremely good money and get to travel anywhere. Still, I can't get rid of this feeling that I need to be doing more. I just need time to figure out what I want to do with my life. And I want to be a better mate to you."

"You don't need to change anything about yourself, Tiff. I love you just as you are. By the way, last night, I couldn't keep my eyes off of you. You looked amazing in that dress."

"Your date didn't look so bad herself."

"We're just friends. She was passing through Atlanta, and I invited her to the ceremony. I didn't think she would actually show up."

Our conversation was going well until reality set in: I was heading off to Costa Rica tomorrow.

Malik begged me to stay until September as we had initially planned. But I told him I needed this time to get myself together.

"I don't think you understand—I don't want to be apart from you. I need you to be right here by my side."

"I don't either."

"Then just stay, and we'll go down to Costa Rica together in September."

"I just need some time to myself and time to get my mind right."

"Are you having second thoughts about us?"

"No, baby. Not at all. I just need some head space, and I know I can't do it in Atlanta."

"Well, you definitely can't leave tomorrow. We have too much time to make up for, and there's not enough in a day for us to catch up on everything."

So, I agreed to stay for an additional month.

***

That month came and went in a flash. Before heading off to Costa Rica, Malik and I spent nearly every waking moment together.

I had brunch with the girls at our favorite spot a couple of times, too, and they were happy for Malik and me. Even Hannah, the skeptic, was elated that we had moved past our problems. Roxanne couldn't understand why I was leaving at all, but I told her that I was going to use this time apart wisely. I was hoping to look for other employment opportunities, but mostly, I needed to get my mind together.

"Let me know if you see any employment opportunities for me," Roxanne asked.

"You're still working, right?" Hannah asked.

"Yes, I am, but it's only a matter of time before my position is eliminated."

"How so?"

"There's a movement spearheaded by right-wing lobbyists advocating for employers nationwide to prioritize inclusion and diversity efforts, in that order. The word 'equity' has been removed to avoid any appearance of preferential treatment for any one group. They claim this 'levels the playing field,' but that's a blatant lie. The CEO sent out a mass email suggesting that DEI is not necessary or critical for business, which explains why the entire time in this position, I felt like I was drowning from day one, and everyone sat back and chose not to do anything or even offer a life preserver. Dammit, I'm ready for something new and better."

"So, what are your plans?" Hannah asked.

Roxanne shrugged. "I might just go back to what I know best—accounting. Next month, I start IVF treatments," she screeched in excitement.

"Oh my God! That's wonderful," I said. "I'm so happy for you."

"Pray that everything goes well for us."

Hannah reached across the table and gave her arm a reassuring squeeze. "Everything will be fine. I'm really happy for you and Scott."

"Well, enough about me. How's the job coming along for you?"

Hannah frowned. "The usual microaggressions. They took me off a few stories and handed them to less experienced reporters. I was all set to interview Kamala Harris during her campaign visit to town. After preparing thoroughly, they reassigned the story to a young, blonde reporter who had only been at the station for two weeks. It was clear she was in over her head—she asked the Vice President if she carried hot sauce in her purse."

Our mouths dropped in shock. "What did Kamala say?" I asked.

"She laughed and said no. The interview was painful to watch. Everyone in the newsroom was stunned."

Roxanne asked, "What did the news director say?"

"Well, the soundbite went viral. Practically, every station in the country ran the interview. Some of the headlines read, 'Unlike Hillary, Kamala prefers it less spicy.' Girls, it even made it in the Shaderoom."

"What?" I exclaimed.

"It turns out the reporter's dad is high up in the local party. I was so upset and in tears that I went home early. I blamed it on a throbbing migraine. I'd wanted that opportunity so badly. This was a chance to show everyone that I have what it takes to be on network news, but this job has disappointed me so many times that nothing surprises me anymore."

Roxanne sighed, then said, "Aside from that, everything is going well with me and my honey, Mike. He is so supportive, and he always has my back."

***

Malik stayed with me as long as he could before I had to go through TSA. I was more in love with him then than ever before.

As I flew home, I stared out the window, longing to be with him, watching the clouds drift by.

Our relationship was so different than it had become before. We were laughing again and enjoying each other's company. We rented an RV and stayed a week at an RV site in Tennessee, where the cell phone reception was poor and at times, there was no signal at all. And the best part was that it didn't bother Malik in the least.

He was so attentive. We went fishing and even did some hiking, taking an eight-mile trail and spending time frolicking under a beautiful, calming waterfall.

I could've done without the hike, as I was afraid we would get lost, having watched too many Lifetime movies. But I was confident that Malik knew the way back home.

Malik's love for nature and the outdoors was fascinating to see. He opened up more about his childhood and shared stories of going out camping in North Carolina and Panama with his dad. While his dad was strict, he never wavered when it came to supporting Malik and his sister.

The bond we created these past weeks was stronger than ever, and I dreamed of becoming Mrs. Walker one day.

We talked about marriage and wondered what our children would look like. Admittedly, all this marriage talk made me nervous as hell. Would I be a good mother and wife to Malik? I still had my own personal goals to fulfill, and Malik had been encouraging me to work on my photography more. It had been close to a year since I last picked up my camera.

As the plane soared higher, I began to think about how I would use this time to rediscover my passion for photography, practice more yoga for balance, and attend therapy to find clarity in my thoughts. I wanted to return to Malik as the best version of myself, ready to embrace our life together without any lingering doubts.

Costa Rica was not just a getaway; it was home and an opportunity for me to reconnect with my dreams and ensure that my love for Malik was secure and on a solid foundation.

Chapter 21

Krush Groove

I arrived shortly before midnight and made sure to text everyone to let them know I had arrived home safely.

As soon as I opened Maverick's carrier, he darted through the villa like a madman. He was happy to be back, too.

Fresh flowers and a bowl of mangos, star fruit, passion, and a few other exotic fruits adorned the kitchen table, a thoughtful touch left by Malik through my cleaning lady.

The sweetness of the ripe fruit and the exotic floral scents filled the air, creating a comforting welcome. I took a deep breath, savoring the moment. It was good to be home.

***

I began my day with the routine early walk on the beach with Maverick, letting the warm water caress my feet and the morning sun warm my skin. The fresh scent of saltwater permeated the air, and I took long moments to simply breathe it in. A few times, I stretched my arms as far as I could, hoping to release any toxins from my inner spirit that could potentially affect my day.

I was missing Malik. I thought about every conversation we had, his laughter and his touch. Memories of our moments together these past weeks filled my mind, and I longed to be with him. I sent him a morning text, telling him how much I loved him and that I couldn't wait to be by his side. He replied that he couldn't wait either.

Work kept me super busy. It was the start of a new fiscal year, and several projects were already underway. As the senior software engineer, I was the lead on most of those projects and consistently had to head up meetings among my team members.

Following my morning walk, I had back-to-back team calls before finally meeting with my new therapist through telehealth.

I sat comfortably on my lounge chair on the patio with Maverick stretched out on the pavers as I poured my heart out to my therapist, Jane.

I guessed she was from Central America, and I was right. She was delighted that I made that connection. She was born in Honduras, a Garifuna and raised mostly in Brooklyn. She had a tawny complexion and shoulder-length sisterlocks with noticeable strands of gray around her hairline. When she smiled, a gap between her front teeth became visible. She looked to be in her early fifties and in good physical shape.

When she spoke, it was as though she was singing. Her cadence and the melody of her voice were soothing. Her accent was a blend of her Garifuna heritage and East New York upbringing. This made our conversations feel comfortable and not imposing in the least. At times, I felt like I was talking to a long-lost friend.

"Tell me, why have you chosen to see a therapist?" Jane asked.

"I've been feeling overwhelmed."

"How long have you been feeling this way?"

"Since my friend died, or maybe even before."

"Tell me what's happening."

Before I could say another word, tears welled up in my eyes, and I began to sob. I just didn't know where to start. All I knew was that my life felt like it was in shambles.

Maverick jumped into my lap and started licking my face. "I'm okay, Maverick," I said, trying to reassure him while I directed him to return to his place on the ground.

"Take your time, Tiffany," Jane gently encouraged.

"I have a lot going on. My best friend Elena died, and I ran into an ex-boyfriend from college and that caused a major problem in my current relationship."

After an hour of sharing with her some of my issues, she suggested that I take some time to process my emotions and consider journaling to sort through my feelings. She also recommended setting up a few more sessions to dive deeper into each issue and develop a plan to address them.

Before the session ended, she encouraged me to do something today that I've been wanting to do for myself. So, I decided to go out and spend the afternoon taking photos.

I pulled out my camera that had been stowed away in a closet and took Maverick to our happy place—the beach.

I began snapping photos of him, and I threw a tennis ball into the water. Maverick raced after it, catching it just before it was swept away by the waves. The eye-catching photos captured Maverick practically in mid-air, grabbing hold of the ball. I couldn't wait to show the photos to Malik and Jane.

***

I woke up around 2:00 AM to what seemed like a hundred notifications from Langston on my cell phone. He wanted to meet up for lunch and said he missed me. I replied immediately with anger and disgust, telling him never to contact me again.

"I'm sorry I didn't reach out to you sooner," he wrote. "I was busy handling some business affairs outside of the country."

I responded, "You're a liar, and if you continue to reach out to me, I will call your wife." This threat worked and the messages stopped immediately. I then blocked him on LinkedIn and on my cell phone.

I couldn't wait for daylight so I could video call Roxanne and Hannah to tell them about the nightmare experience, and that's just what I did first thing the next day. The girls were in total shock as I recounted my early morning fiasco with Langston.

"He's obsessed with you," Hannah exclaimed.

"How do you feel about it all?" Roxanne asked.

"A bit shaken up, but I feel better now that it's over."

Roxanne asked, "Are you planning to tell Malik what happened?"

"No, I handled it, and it's over. Done. I blocked Langston on every platform I can think of."

Roxanne hummed in disapproval, and Hannah said, "I agree with Roxanne. I think you should tell Malik in case anything else happens."

"No way! I don't want Malik to feel any kind of way about this situation. I handled it, and that's it."

Roxanne had an anxious look on her face. "Well, I'm heading into my doctor's office, so got to go."

"And I'm on my way to my pilates class," Hannah announced.

"How's the IVF going?" I asked Roxanne.

"They gave me some medicine to suppress my period, and next, they'll give me medicine to produce more eggs. I pray that my geriatric eggs are good."

"They will be," I assured her. "Oh, my goodness, this is actually happening!" I broke out in a song, swaying side to side. "I can't wait to host a baby shower for you."

Roxanne laughed. "Alright, ladies, I really have to go. I'll chat with you later."

Malik called just minutes after I ended our joint call while driving to his office. "Hey baby, how's it going? I love those photos of you and Maverick on the beach. You looked hot."

"You like them?"

"Hell, yes."

"Oh, thank you, baby. I'm going to go live with my website and blog soon. I just want to take a few more photos first."

Malik was wearing his stylish Ray-Bans and a gray polo shirt. He had a fresh fade, and I just wanted to hold him tight. I missed him so much.

"Okay, honey, I'm about to pump some gas. I'm in the rough part of the city and need to focus. I'll call you later. Oh, wait. You received a card in the mail from someone. There was no return address."

"Okay. Thanks, babe."

I went into panic mode. I couldn't believe this was happening, and a few hours later, I received another email from Langston from another account confirming that he sent a card.

Hi, Tiffany,

I hope this email finds you well. There's not enough time in the day to express how much I've missed you. Your smile and touch lighten my world. I'm sorry I didn't get in touch with you sooner, but life got in the way. I drove by your place several times, hoping I could catch up with you. Did you receive my card? I made sure to include some photos of us from the wedding. That night was magical and unforgettable. I hope we can meet up soon.

Love xoxo
Langston

Frantic, I called Jane in tears.

"I want you to take a deep breath," she said, and I started breathing slowly and calmly as she suggested.

"Are you in danger? Do you need immediate help?" she asked.

"No." I then told her how Langston had been in contact with me. "He'll do or use anything to destroy what I have with Malik."

"I want you to give Langston a call and let him know that you have moved on. Let him know you would appreciate it if he didn't call you anymore."

"I've already told him that."

"Yes, but by text. You may have a better chance of getting through to him by phone. He needs to hear in your voice that you're serious. Be firm with him so that he understands."

"Jane, thank you for taking my call. One more thing, should I tell Malik about what's going on?"

"I believe you should tell him everything. You don't want to hold any secrets at this stage of your relationship."

***

I tossed and turned all night. I wasn't sure what was troubling me. Was I afraid of Langston somehow steering me away from Malik? Sometimes, I felt like Langston had a strong grip on me, though my love for Malik was more solid than ever.

As Jane suggested, I tried calling Langston. It took four times before he finally called me back.

"Hey, babe. I'm so happy to hear from you. I knew you would change your mind."

"Langston, I need you to listen to me. I don't want you to contact me anymore. What we had is over. I am in love with Malik, and besides that, you're married."

"Let me explain."

"No. You don't need to explain anything to me. Do us all a favor and stop contacting me."

"I thought I was the one that got away."

"I'm happy with the life I've chosen."

"That's not what you've been telling me."

"Listen, my life is in Costa Rica. There is nothing that I can do for you anymore. It's over between us. If you reach out to me again, I *will* call your wife," I said firmly.

"And tell my wife what? Huh? Tell her what? That you fucked her husband in a closet at a wedding that she attended with me."

"Through no fault of mine. I didn't know she existed. So, yeah."

"Or maybe the narcissist in you didn't want to know she existed. You were too busy wanting me for your damn self. Did you tell your man that while he sat at the table with his bros, downing tequila shots, his favorite girl was riding my dick?" When I didn't respond, he added, "Not even three months ago, you were running around town desperately looking for me. You play a lot of fucked up games, Tiff. This hot one minute and cold the next is exhausting. As soon as he pisses you off and you're not getting the attention you want, you'll be running back to me."

The call ended abruptly. I said "hello" a few times, then stared at my cell phone, trying to figure out what happened. I wasn't sure if I had accidentally hung up on him or if he'd had enough and purposely hung up on me. Maybe his battery had died, or the call had dropped. Or perhaps he'd heard his wife coming into the room.

He didn't call back, and that was a relief. However, a few weeks later, I did hear from his wife. She called, knowing exactly who I was, and it strangely felt as though he'd put her up to calling me.

"You've been the third person in my marriage for years," she said. Before I could explain that I had only one encounter with Langston, she continued. "He never got over you. He always talked about how smart and beautiful you were. He even wanted to name our firstborn after you, but I adamantly refused."

The conversation grew more awkward by the minute. "Why are you telling me all of this?"

"I want to thank you for giving my husband the closure he needed. Our marriage has never been better. Even our kids noticed the change in him."

"I'm sorry, I have a work call to hop on," I said, wanting to end this awkward conversation.

"That's fine. Thank you for taking my call and… Thank you again."

I met with Jane and told her about the call with Langston's wife. I told her how I felt somehow responsible for the turmoil in their marriage. Jane listened intently, and her brow furrowed with concern.

'You can't blame yourself for his choices," she said gently. "People have to take responsibility for their own actions. It sounds like his wife is relieved, and their marriage is stronger now. Maybe it really was the closure he needed."

I nodded, trying to absorb her words. "I hope you're right. It's just hard not to feel guilty."

"It's natural to feel that way," Jane reassured me. "But remember, you're not responsible for the past. Focus on moving forward."

I took a deep breath, grateful for her support. "Thanks, Jane. I needed to hear that."

"Anytime," she replied with a warm smile. "You're not alone in this."

Later, I told Malik most of what happened. He didn't want to hear any more and especially didn't want to know where our escapade took place. I could see the frustration in his eyes as he cut me off mid-sentence.

"I don't need the details," he said firmly. "Let's just move on from this."

I nodded, understanding his feelings. "Alright. I won't bring it up again."

It was clear Malik wanted to put the past behind us, and I had to respect that.

Therapy was going well. The anxiety that had taken refuge in my mind was no longer a problem, and even work demands didn't seem as overwhelming. I made good use of my free time by simply enjoying life and not worrying about tomorrow or what it might hold for me. I just wanted to be present and embrace a positive outlook on life.

I even found time to create content for my social media platforms and on my website. I was stunned how, in such a short time, I grew a following—mostly women, consisting of Gen Z and Gen X expats. I even dealt with the trolls from time to time.

Thanks to Jane, I found my voice and a healthy balance that worked for me. I never imagined that spending a few hours a week on my mental health would make such a difference in my life.

There was no more haze, and I could finally see the light at the end of the tunnel.

Chapter 22

Hurricane

I longed for Malik. We missed each other so much that most nights, one of us would fall asleep on the phone. I hung on to every word he said, counting the days until we could be in each other's arms again. And the impending storm didn't make it easier.

Malik was deeply concerned about my well-being as Category Four Hurricane Ernesto loomed on the horizon. It was predicted to be the biggest hurricane Costa Rica had faced in forty years. The situation was so dire that the U.S. offered to send aid and resources in advance to help mitigate potential disaster.

Malik's office was closed, and evacuation orders were issued for everyone while his parents were safe with his sister in the States. Malik begged me to come to Atlanta to ride out the storm, but by the time I looked into it, all the flights were either sold out or canceled.

An official from the consulate's office knocked on my door, suggesting that I evacuate, but pets were not allowed in the shelter, so I decided to stay put and ride out the storm with Maverick.

As the hurricane drew near our shores, I stayed glued to CNN news, hoping it would pivot in a different direction. I had not heard from Malik all day, which was odd, especially after he promised he would stay in touch as best as he possibly could throughout the storm. I tried calling him numerous times to no avail.

In the beginning, the weather was eerily calm, with a cool breeze that made sleeping easy—the calm before the storm. The breeze swayed the trees back and forth. As each hour went by, the gust of wind gradually picked up like a relentless force, battering windows and moving anything in its way. Trees had fallen, and the seawater rising steadily had traveled past the embankment and onto the streets, giving the appearance of a city submerged. The power in the villa flickered for about an hour, and then, eventually, we went into complete darkness. A few hours later, the generator turned on.

Maverick and I cuddled together in my bed. I prayed for the storm to pass quickly, but the hours dragged on, each one stretching into what felt like an eternity. I tried to stay awake, but exhaustion eventually overtook me as the full fury of Ernesto unleashed itself outside.

Finally, the hurricane began making its way toward the Gulf of Mexico. The heavy winds started to subside, and the rain lessened to an intense tropical storm, but the scene outside was no less unsettling.

The streets were flooded, cars overturned, and debris had been scattered everywhere. Despite the fallen trees strewn across the roads and manicured lawns, the villa remained intact.

Massive waves crashed into the shoreline. Families clung to anything they could find to stay safe—some perched atop cars, others braving the floodwaters by walking, swimming, or even managing to drive through the chaos. I took a few photos to capture the aftermath and to later share with my family and friends.

I felt helpless, knowing there was nothing I could do, and I sat by the window in tears. I had never experienced anything like this before, the closest being the time I was stranded in a few inches of snow, and even that paled in comparison.

I woke up to several missed calls from Mike and Hannah. It took a few tries, but I finally managed to connect with them. "Hi, Hannah."

She immediately called out, "Babe, Tiffany is on the phone!" I heard Mike saying something in the background, but his voice was faint, and the connection was poor. However, I caught Malik's name.

"Have you guys heard from Malik?" I asked, feeling a sudden unease. There was a long silence on their end. "Hello? Are you there?"

Finally, Hannah spoke, but her voice was heavy with emotion. "Yes, we're here," she said with a deep sigh. "Are you safe?"

"Yes," I replied and started to describe the aftermath of the storm. But Hannah interrupted me.

"Listen closely. Malik hopped on a flight to Costa Rica. He wanted to surprise you and wait out the storm with you."

"He did what?" I asked, my heart skipping a beat. "When? Where is he?"

Mike took the phone, and I heard Hannah crying in the background. My heart started to pound. "Malik called me to let me know he landed safely," Mike began, "and that he was taking a local bus into town to get to where you are."

"Okay, so he's on his way? Right, Mike?"

There was a pause. "I'm afraid I have some bad news."

My stomach dropped. "What do you mean by bad news? Where's Malik? I need to go get him."

"The embassy contacted me," Mike said, his voice strained. "There was an accident, and Malik may have been among the people on a bus… Everyone was killed, Tiff."

"Wait. Are you saying Malik is dead?"

"It's not for certain. He was seen boarding the bus. That's all I know for sure."

I dropped to my knees, and the cell phone slipped from my hand as I let out a heart-wrenching wail. I couldn't believe what I was hearing.

"He can't be dead!" I screamed, pleading for this to be some horrible mistake. "God, help me," I repeated over and over. "Please don't do this to me now. In the background, I heard Hannah calling my name, but her voice seemed distant, drowned out by my overwhelming grief.

I was in complete shock and couldn't move. I didn't know what to do or how to process what I had just heard. I began to pray, and I begged God to bring him home whole, and I promised I would be a better person.

I knew I was praying for a miracle, but I refused to give up hope. I pulled out every photo I could find of us and scattered them on my bed. I needed Malik to be right here with me. I was desperate to have him beside me. How could I go on without this man? Malik and I were made for each other.

I stopped answering calls. At first, I answered every call that came through, thinking it might be Malik calling me to tell me that he was alive and well. But after the third call, if it wasn't from his number, I just couldn't. It was too much to handle.

I became enraged and couldn't control my emotions. I cried myself to sleep and woke up hoping that this was a nightmare, but I was quickly reminded that it wasn't when I looked outside and saw brown water flowing through the streets.

I made myself a cup of tea, and the idea to open Elena's box came to me. Jane and I had recently talked about me opening Elena's box, but I wasn't sure at the time if I was ready to deal with those raw emotions. Jane suggested that I look at it more for healing rather than a painful reminder. I was skeptical, but now, it seemed like the right time. I needed to hear from Elena.

While I sat at the kitchen table, the steam from my tea and the soothing aroma of coconut milk, chamomile, honey and ginger filled the air around me. I gently sipped on the hot tea as I placed the worn box in front of me.

A subtle and familiar scent—a hint of jasmine, lavender and something floral—instantly brought back memories of Elena. I felt her presence around me, and fresh tears filled my eyes.

With trembling hands, I opened the box. Inside sat some beautiful jewelry made of ivory and brass that Elena had brought back from Ghana and huge gold hoops. These were the hoops I borrowed from her every time I was in Atlanta.

On a handwritten note, she wrote, "These hoops are for those days you need to be reminded how fine you are." I couldn't help but smile.

She left me with a camel-colored tunic blouse, an off-white fitted blazer and denim jeans. I also found a cream and gold jumpsuit designed by a local designer and a pair of Chanel spandrels. The outfits were perfect and had Elena written all over them. She had an impeccable style. I was thankful for everything that she had given me, but I was eager to see her face and hear her words of wisdom.

I placed my laptop in front of me and entered the private code for Vimeo. Then, I watched the video she made for me, which was twenty minutes in length.

The video opened with Elena sitting on her bed, and the camera zoomed in close. I had forgotten just how frail she had become, but cancer could never take away her stunning beauty.

Her sunken eyes stared directly into the camera as if she were speaking straight to me. She paused, often mid-sentence, to sip some water.

With every word, she expressed how much she loved me and how proud she was of me. She admired my courage to pick up and move to Costa Rica. She urged me to let love run its course, not to fear it but to embrace it. She also told me that I needed to learn to live life on its terms.

I didn't fully grasp what she meant until she explained. "If you're driving down a road and encounter a roadblock, accept it and find an alternate route." Was I not living on life's terms? Was my ego to blame? My resistance to the roadblock stemmed from expecting things to go a certain way and not being able to accept it and move on.

Her words resonated with me so profoundly that a sudden chill went through my entire body. I felt the desire to bathe, to clean up and to get my life in order. Most of all, I knew I needed to come to terms with the fact that Malik could be dead.

I reached out to Jane to fill her in on what was happening. "How are you feeling?" she asked.

"I have mixed emotions. I want to accept that he could be dead, but another part of me doesn't want to give up. I just can't. I love Malik, and I don't know if I can live without him."

Jane sighed softly. "Tiffany, it's okay to feel conflicted. You're going through something unimaginable. It's natural to hold on to hope, especially when you love someone so deeply."

I swallowed hard, the lump in my throat making it difficult to speak. I couldn't stop crying. "But what if he's really gone, Jane?"

There was a brief silence before she responded, speaking firmly yet with compassion. "One step at a time, Tiffany. Right now, you don't have to make any decisions or force yourself to accept anything. Just breathe. Let yourself feel whatever comes without judgment."

I closed my eyes, letting her words sink in. "Thank you, Jane. I just… I just don't know how to do this."

"You're not alone in this," she said gently. "You have your friends and family, and you're stronger than you realize."

I really wanted to believe her, but the ache in my heart was far too deep, and I wouldn't allow it. "I hope you're right," I whispered.

"You'll get through this," she reassured me. "One day at a time."

When I ended the Zoom call, I got on my knees and prayed, allowing God's words to sink in. I knew the days ahead would be filled with uncertainty, but for now, I clung to hope that somehow, somewhere, Malik was still alive.

By late that day, the flood waters had nearly receded, and the grounds crew had already started clearing the fallen trees and debris left behind by the storm.

The airport had resumed operations, and Mike, Hannah, and Malik's family were set to head to Costa Rica on Monday. I was looking forward to spending some quality time with my bestie, Hannah. To keep myself busy, I started cleaning the inside of the villa while listening to Yolanda Adams' classic, "The Battle is the Lord's." Later, I cooled down to a classic Brandy Full Moon album. It was just what I needed to clear my mind and relax.

Maverick had truly become our protector. I watched him as he pranced around the villa and noticed that he wasn't his normal, playful self. I wondered if he could sense something was wrong.

I rubbed his belly a few times and reminded myself that we were off our morning ritual, which was spending time at the beach. I made sure to place Maverick's pillow inside Malik's T-shirt. Maverick dragged that pillow everywhere in the house and even fell asleep on top of it.

Chapter 23

The Pursuit of Happiness

I woke believing Malik was out there somewhere and that God would bring him back home. I wasn't sure if I was getting closer to the truth or further away, but I held on to my faith.

Tomorrow was a big day as Malik's parents, Hannah and Mike, were flying in, and we were scheduled to meet with the authorities. Before then, I needed to clear my mind, and the perfect place to do that was on the beach.

It was a beautiful morning, and Maverick and I were eager to be outdoors. The beach was serene, with the sun shining so bright that it reflected off the water, casting a warm glow. I set up my towel and large umbrella, then made myself comfortable, hoping to get some more rest.

Meanwhile, Maverick was his usual curious self, roaming around and discovering new things. I kept a close eye on him to make sure he stayed safe. Rottweilers were not a common breed in Costa Rica, and on the black market, they could easily be sold for thousands of dollars.

My Maverick was extremely friendly, and I would not want to test his loyalty because food of any kind, including a chicken bone, could steer him away.

I pulled out my cell phone to see if there were any updates from Mike and grabbed a bottle of water from my tote bag and a pack of Skittles to munch on, but then I noticed Maverick was gone. I called out to him several times, but he didn't appear.

I started looking for him, and in the distance, I saw someone had caught Maverick's attention, and they were playing together in the sand. As they started running toward me, I realized it was Malik. I couldn't identify his height and stature from that distance at first, but as recognition hit, I couldn't believe my eyes. My heart started pumping a mile a minute, hoping I was right, and in my rush to reach him, I tripped and fell into the sand.

I never cried so hard in my life as I did that day.

Malik looked disheveled with his bookbag on his back, very unlike his usual put-together self. He grabbed hold of me and held me in his arms, whispering how much he loved me over and over.

"Malik, you're alive," I blurted out.

"Babe, of course I am."

"We haven't heard from you in two days."

"I had no cell connection, and the phones in the office weren't working."

"Didn't you get on a bus?"

"Yes, I did."

"Did you know there was an accident and people died on that bus?" Malik turned to me in shock and suddenly became sad by the news.

"Wow, no, I didn't know." It took him a few seconds to gather his thoughts. "My parents must be worried sick about me. I did get on the bus, but I got off at around the third stop. I gave up my seat to a father who boarded the bus with his pregnant wife and four children. There were no more seats left, so I offered mine to him and then hitched a ride. The closest the driver could get me was about a quarter of a mile from the office. I got there as fast as I could and waited out the hurricane, sleeping on the couch. I ate some crackers and drank bottled water that was in the fridge."

"Come. Sit down and tell me the rest."

He nodded, and we sat side by side on my towel as he picked up his story. "When the hurricane passed through, I paid a driver to get me as close to you as he could before the rising tide made travel impossible. The water was rising quickly, and we got caught in the middle of it. I had to walk the rest of the way."

"Babe, I didn't want to think the worst, but…" I said as I began to cry. "I tried so hard not to give up hope."

"I was worried about you too and mad at myself for not getting home sooner. I wanted to surprise you. I didn't want you to be alone in the storm. The last thing I wanted to do was to have you worried about me. Are you okay?"

"Yes, and so grateful that you're here."

"Well, let's go home. I'm starving. Plus, I'm soaking wet, and I need to get out of these clothes."

Minutes later, as I began preparing dinner, Malik called home to speak with his parents. He put them on speaker, and I could literally hear his mom wailing at the sound of Malik's voice. The excitement and raw emotion in their voices were evident—they were understandably overjoyed that he had made it home safely.

The conversation flowed between English and Spanish, with his parents mostly speaking to him in Spanish. As they were saying goodbye, I heard his mom say, *"Dios te bendiga, mi hijo,"* which I knew translated to "God Bless you, my son."

Later, he spoke to Mike, whose voice trembled at the initial sound of Malik's voice. As they ended the call, I heard Mike say, "I love you, bro."

Malik, his voice cracking with emotion, replied, "I love you too, cuz. See you tomorrow."

***

We had so much to celebrate, and Malik's parents planned a small dinner party at their home to welcome our guests from out of town. To my surprise, Roxanne, along with Scott and even Greg, had flown in with Hannah and Mike. I couldn't stop crying when I saw all of our friends, who had been ready and willing to join a search and rescue mission to find Malik.

We spent most of the evening laughing at childhood stories shared by Malik's parents and sister. His mom even pulled out the family photo album.

Malik could be seen in one of the photos wearing a red, white and blue jumper with suspenders and sporting a little hat on top of a burgeoning afro—holding his sister's hand. He looked so adorable. Malik definitely inherited his charm from his dad and his compassionate nature from his beautiful mom.

The entire house was decorated with lush tropical flowers and scented candles, creating a stunning oasis. A few times, I caught Malik staring at me. He seemed nervous, and I wasn't sure if he was worried that his parents were oversharing or if something else was bothering him.

I winked to reassure him that everything was going to be okay. Then, Malik began talking about me and our relationship.

"It was love at first sight for me. Not sure if that was the case for Tiffany. Before I could ask her for her telephone number, she ran out of the store."

Embarrassed, I quickly explained, "I was late for a work call."

Everyone laughed, and Malik added, "I am so blessed to have an incredible woman like Tiffany by my side. She's been nothing but a breath of fresh air. If we learned anything this past week, life is too short," he said as his voice began to tremble. Malik held my hand and looked directly into my eyes. "Tiffany, I love you so much."

"I love you too," I replied, my heart swelling with anxiety.

"You are my best friend, and I want to spend every waking moment with you." Malik suddenly got down on one knee, and the room filled with gasps of surprise, eyes widening with anticipation.

He pulled out a stunning pear-shaped diamond ring, and instantly, there wasn't a dry eye in the room.

I was in complete shock, like a deer caught in headlights. The expression on my face must have said it all because it took me a moment to realize he was proposing.

"Yes, yes, I'll marry you!" I screamed. I was not only stunned by the proposal and the huge rock but also by the fact that he wanted to get married in less than twenty-four hours, which he outlined the moment my shock died down.

"Don't worry," Malik said with a reassuring smile before turning to Hannah.

"We have everything you need," she assured me, "including a wedding dress, shoes, and even hair and makeup."

"But…where are we going to get married?"

Malik waved a hand. "Right here at my parents' estate, on the beach."

I turned to Hannah and Roxanne. "Wait a minute. You guys were in on this?" I was still trying to process everything.

"Since everyone is here, why not?" Malik grinned.

From across the room, Hannah jumped in. "I went to my friend's showroom in Buckhead, and she pulled a few dresses that I knew would look perfect on you."

Malik's sister added, "And my makeup artist and hairstylist are on standby for tomorrow, and as you know, our mom is a retired seamstress. So, if any adjustments are needed, she'll take care of it."

***

Before the dinner party could end, the girls and I unpacked an assortment of dresses. I was anxious about finding the right fit, even though I knew I'd be just as happy marrying Malik in jeans. But I couldn't help thinking about the day we'd show our children photos of this special moment, so I had to look fabulous.

I finally settled for the perfect dress for the wedding—a stunning couture gown, floral white, off-the-shoulder, and form-fitting. I tried on a few, but everyone, including Malik's mom, raved over that one. It had a modern elegance to it that could easily make it a wedding dress.

Malik's mom let me borrow her veil, which matched perfectly with the gown, the jewelry and right down to the shoes. I had hair and makeup confirmed for 10:00 AM and felt like I could relax a bit.

***

Dressed in pink matching pajamas and white hair bonnets, courtesy of Hannah, the girls and I stayed up late laughing and talking, making ourselves comfortable on a California king-size bed in Malik's parents' guest house.

"I can't believe I'm getting married tomorrow!" I screeched.

"Bitch, we can't either," Roxanne said, and we all burst into laughter.

I said, "Alright, ladies, let's make a toast. Can we all agree we've finally exhaled?"

"Cheers, cheers!" Hannah raised her glass of ginger ale.

"We've got to get you and Mike to say 'I do,' too," I added.

"We almost eloped a few weeks ago," she admitted.

"What stopped you?"

"Girl, I'm a Virgo," she replied with a roll of her eyes. "I need at least a year to plan my wedding. I can't do last-minute things like you and Malik."

Then, Hannah teased, "So, you're Gloria from *Waiting to Exhale*, now?"

Even though we were barely in high school when the iconic movie *Waiting to Exhale* hit the theaters, we'd watched it a million times at CC-4. Over the years, we'd come to identify with the characters so closely that we'd constantly find ourselves debating who the true Savannah, Robin, Bernadine or Gloria in our group was as if the film was a mirror reflecting our lives, especially since we had now reached the characters' ages in the movie.

"I'm Lela Rochon's character," Roxanne said.

"She played Robin," I chimed in. None of us could ever remember that character's name, only the name of the actress who played the role in the movie. "And I guess I'm Savannah."

"No, Elena was Savannah. And you know I'm Bernadine, right?" Hannah added.

"Yes, we know," Roxanne and I said in unison, laughing.

Hannah suddenly started acting out one of the scenes in the movie. "No, Bernadine, you can't start your catering business this year. Why don't you wait a few years, huh? Yeah, don't start it right now. Wait one, two, three years. I need you to be the fuckin background to my foreground!"

We all started laughing as we knew the words verbatim in the movie, especially scenes with Savannah and Bernadine.

I noticed Roxanne hadn't touched any of the champagne. "Why are you not drinking?" She had a smirk on her face. "Wait," I gasped. "You're pregnant?"

Roxanne grinned, stood and revealed her new baby bump. Hannah and I screamed with joy.

"How far along are you?" I asked.

"Sixteen weeks."

"You've hidden it so well!" I rubbed her belly.

"Have you told anyone at work?"

"Not yet, but I did tell my supervisor that I wanted to return to the accounting department. She denied my request but promised I'd get the support I need moving forward," Roxanne explained.

"Well, that's great, right?"

"Yes, especially now that Kamala Harris' campaign is gaining momentum, and we could possibly have our first woman president. They're panicking and restructuring the department to make sure we stay at the forefront of DEI. After I come back from maternity leave, I'll decide whether to stay on or start my own accounting firm. Good thing my husband supports me either way."

Hannah grinned and said, "Well, ladies, I have some news too. I turned in my resignation."

"What? At the news station?" Roxanne asked, surprised.

"Yeah, I was offered an early morning anchor shift on CNN."

"Girl, that's awesome!" I exclaimed.

"Yes. I'm at the network, baby!"

Hannah jumped on the massive bed. "And I'm celebrating one year of sobriety," she added, her grin widening.

"I am so proud of you," I told her.

"Thank you. It hasn't been easy." She choked up. "But I take one day at a time."

"How about you, Tiff?" Roxanne asked.

"Actually, I've been seeing a therapist, and after working out some issues, my job doesn't seem that bad after all. I'm the lead on several projects, and as the most senior on my team, they value my opinion. Still, I definitely enjoy cooking and doing my photography on the side as well. Malik wants me to host an exhibition featuring my photography, and I think I will. I also have plans to publish a cookbook later next year."

"Elena would be proud of us."

"She sure would." Roxanne rubbed her belly and stood. "Well, ladies, I'm going to bed. We have a long day ahead of us. You need your beauty sleep, and so do I. I need to find my man in this fortress. In fact, I'm going to text him to see where he is," she added, lifting her cell phone.

"But he's with the other guys," I told her.

"And? We don't need to sleep apart. We're already married." Seconds later, her phone beeped with an incoming text. "Okay, my honey is coming. I told him the baby and I are tired. My man spoils me rotten," she added with a huge grin.

Hannah and I looked at each other and laughed.

***

I stood in the foyer, gazing into the distant aqua-blue water. Malik appeared nervous as he waited at the altar. His father, who would officiate our wedding, stood beneath the floral archway, holding a Bible.

Malik looked incredibly handsome in his black tuxedo. The patio leading to the ocean had been transformed into a breathtaking backdrop for our ceremony.

Gorgeous flowers had been placed everywhere, just as I desired, and rows of white chairs lined the aisle, filled with about thirty of our closest friends and family.

I slowly walked to the altar while Malik fought back tears. With his eyes locked onto mine, he mouthed, "You are so beautiful."

As we stood gazing into each other's eyes, I couldn't help but reflect on my journey to love. I made a bold move, leaving behind the hustle and grind of New York City for a calmer life in Costa Rica, and there, I found love when I least expected it.

Now, I was stepping into the next chapter of my life, armed with the promise of a glorious future.

~The End~